THE

Freewheeling

Paul DeMarco, Reno's top divorce attorney, could soon find himself at the wrong end of a personal-injury suit. DeMarco, who's earned a reputation for bleeding his clients' former spouses dry in court, crashed into an airport limo in heavy downtown traffic yesterday morning. Although the lawyer's Mercedes hit the limo at low speed, witnesses report that the driver later collapsed on the pavement and paramedics were summoned.

What makes the case interesting is that the injured woman is Melinda Dumas, owner of Advanced Limo and sister of local ranchers Zach and Zane Dumas of the Twin Bar.

DeMarco represented Dumas's ex-husband in a nasty divorce settlement a year ago, so chances are good that Dumas, a single mother of two, will show no mercy now that the courtroom tables are turned.

Although West View Hospital's ER would not release any details of Ms Dumas's condition, *Review* reporters will continue to follow this story closely.

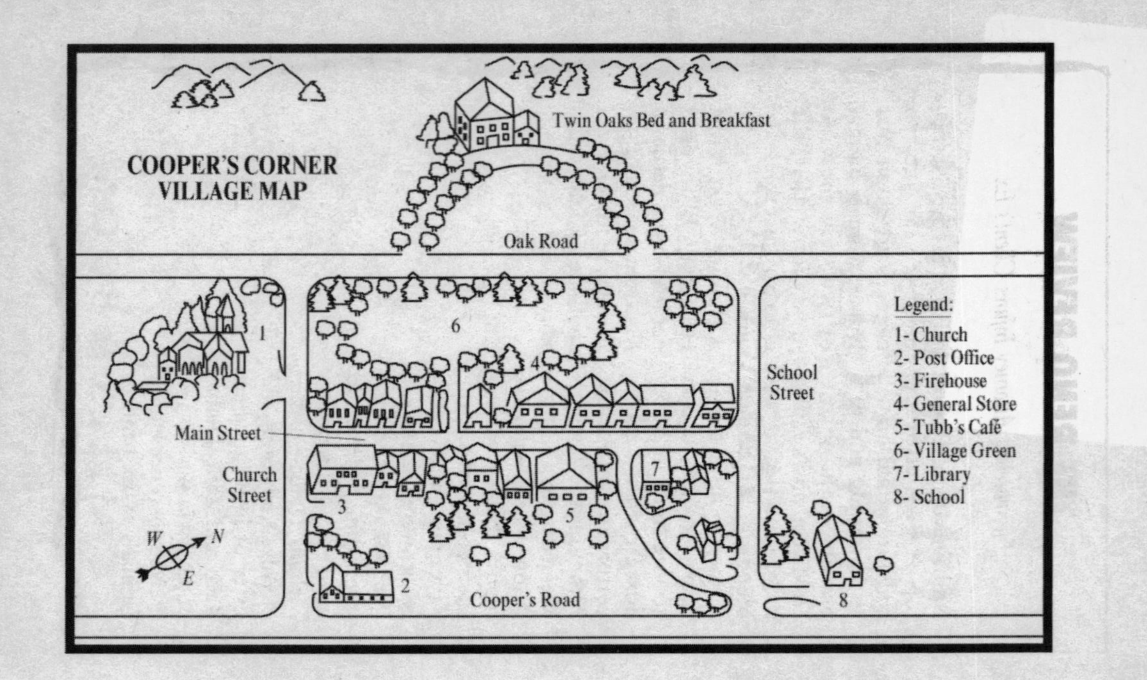
COOPER'S CORNER
VILLAGE MAP
Twin Oaks Bed and Breakfast
Oak Road
Main Street
Church
Street
School
Street
Cooper's Road
W
N
E
1
2
3
4
5
6
7
8
Legend:
1- Church
2- Post Office
3- Firehouse
4- General Store
5- Tubb's Café
6- Village Green
7- Library
8- School

CHARLOTTE MACLAY

The Revenge

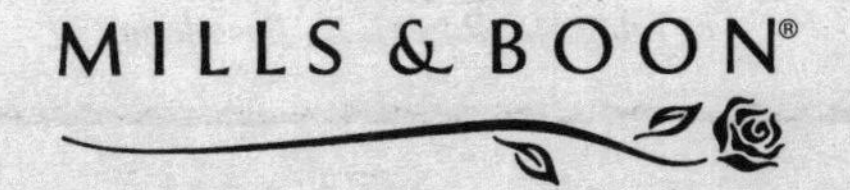

First published in Great Britain 2005
by Harlequin Mills & Boon Limited,
Eton House, 18-24 Paradise Road, Richmond, Surrey TW9 1SR

Charlotte Maclay is acknowledged as the author of this work.

ISBN 0 263 84701 2

142-0905

Printed and bound in Spain
by Litografia Rosés S.A., Barcelona

Dear Reader,

It's been a real delight to be a part of the Cooper's Corner series and have an opportunity to work with so many talented authors. In many cases I've been reading and enjoying their stories for years—as I am sure you have. Other authors are new to me. In all cases, I'm looking forward to seeing how the characters and events evolve, because, just like you, I'm a devoted reader of romance.

My contribution to the series, *The Revenge*, was particularly enjoyable to write. It gave me a chance to have fun exploring once again what "family" means, and redeem an intransigent divorce attorney through the power of love. My hope is that this story will bring a smile to your lips, ease your cares and touch your heart.

Charlotte Maclay

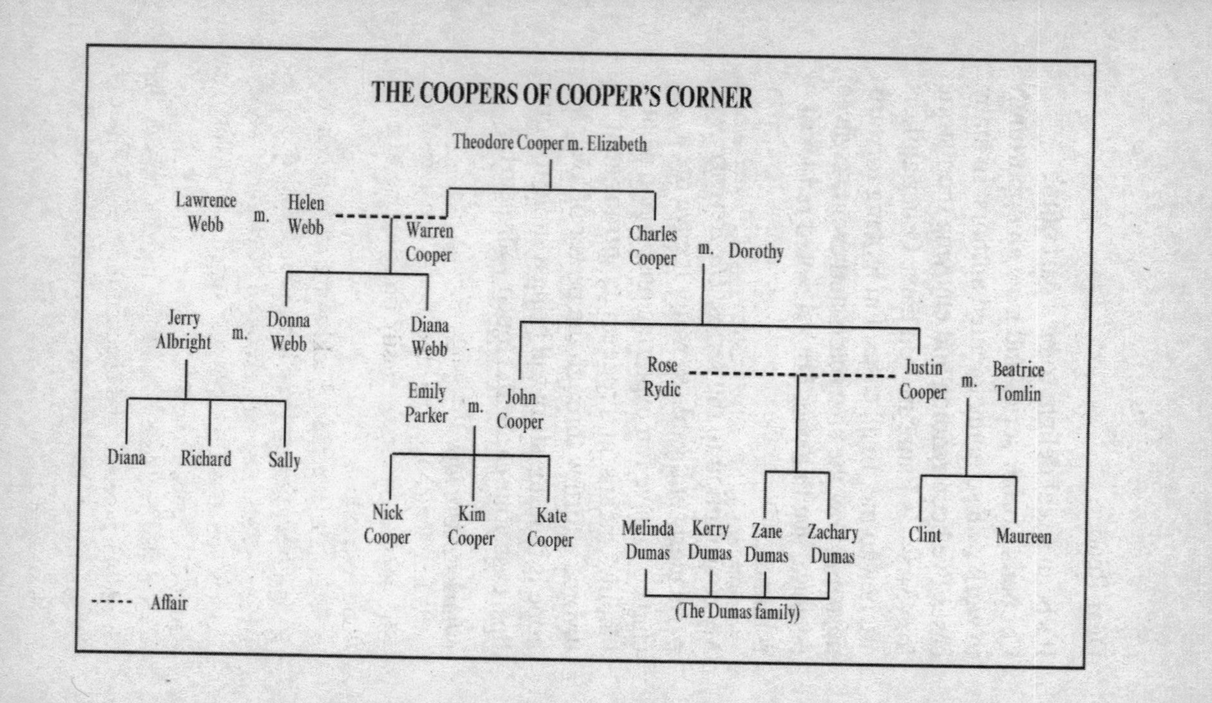
THE COOPERS OF COOPER'S CORNER
Theodore Cooper m. Elizabeth
Lawrence Webb
m.
Helen Webb
Warren Cooper
Charles Cooper
m.
Dorothy
Jerry Albright
m.
Donna Webb
Diana Webb
Diana
Richard
Sally
Emily Parker
m.
John Cooper
Rose Rydic
Justin Cooper
m.
Beatrice Tomlin
Nick Cooper
Kim Cooper
Kate Cooper
Melinda Dumas
Kerry Dumas
Zane Dumas
Zachary Dumas
(The Dumas family)
Clint
Maureen
Affair

CHAPTER ONE

RENO'S DOWNTOWN TRAFFIC let up just enough for Melinda Dumas to ease the limo away from the hotel's taxi curb into the one-way street that fronted the ten-story building. After six weeks with her arm in a cast, due to a fall from her brother's gentlest Arabian mare, it felt good to be behind the wheel again—with a paying client in the back seat.

The morning rush had cars jockeying for position. Wanting to turn left at the next intersection, the best route to the airport, she glanced in her side mirror to see if it was clear to change lanes. Not a chance. She'd have to take the longer—

When she looked up, the signal had turned red. She applied the brake, easily bringing the extended limo to a stop.

Then she felt the whack. Some idiot driver who hadn't been paying attention had rear-ended her.

She swallowed an expletive. Company policy, which she'd written herself, stated no cussing in front of clients. *Damn!*

Not that the jerk behind her had hit her all that hard, she noted as she checked the rearview mirror. A silver-gray 550 Mercedes, for heaven's sake. Probably some dottering old fool on the phone to his stockbroker.

She ground her teeth. She was still going to have to pull over, exchange information and probably have a repair bill for the bumper to worry about—which she would darn well make sure the other driver or his insurance paid. Her deductible was so high it was practically to the moon.

She glanced over her shoulder at her client. ‘‘Are you all right, Mr. Sadmosian?’’ He was a regular customer—an electronic-parts salesman of some sort—and Melinda didn't want to lose him or his firm as clients for her Advanced Limousine Service. She was having enough trouble keeping up with the loan payments on her vehicles as it was. Besides, his tips were good.

‘‘I'm fine, Ms. Dumas, but I am concerned about catching my flight.’’

‘‘Not to worry.’’ With a quick, professional smile, she aimed the limo toward the yellow curb, where she could safely pull over. ‘‘We'll get you there on time.’’

Hopping out of the car, she adjusted her chauffeur's cap on her head and made her way to the sidewalk and the Mercedes, which had pulled in behind her. She was going to get this over with in a hurry.

And then, through the glare on the Mercedes's windshield, she saw the enemy. The man who had brought her so low.

Her ex-husband's shark of an attorney smiled back

at her—the evil villain who had arranged for Orly to pay no alimony. Zip. And only enough child support to cover her children's dental bills. They didn't even have adult teeth yet!

Beneath her breath, Melinda snarled as fiercely as any mountain lion in the surrounding eastern Sierra foothills. She wasn't a vindictive person. Usually. But Paul DeMarco, divorce attorney extraordinaire, had gone one step too far. Now was her chance to get her revenge. Not only for herself but for all the ex-wives he'd no doubt stripped of their rightful support, their self-respect. She'd teach him a lesson.

Clutching her neck, she let out the most pathetic cry she could manage and crumpled in a heap to the sidewalk.

Let Paul DeMarco, big gun of the divorce world, figure out how to defend himself in the biggest, meanest whiplash suit he'd ever seen.

PAUL FLASHED a stern look at his young nephews, who'd been bickering in the back seat of the Mercedes, their youthful wrestling match distracting him just enough that he'd nudged the limo in front of him.

''Boys, separate and stay that way till I tell you otherwise.'' Michael, eight, and Steven, ten, scrambled to comply with his order.

Since the limo had pulled over to the curb, Paul had followed, although he doubted he'd done any damage to its bumper. What surprised him was the woman driver who got out. Her trim body was tucked neatly into a black chauffeur's uniform that failed to disguise the gentle swell of her hips or the attractive curve of her breasts, and her heart-shaped face was framed by short, light-brown hair with natural waves that curled over her ears.

He'd met her before, under circumstances that had been less than conducive to developing a friendly relationship.

Smiling, he reached for the door handle. Their eyes met through the windshield, and he was pleased by the recognition he saw in hers.

And then, as though she'd been given a cue from an offstage director in a high school drama production, she grabbed her neck and took the phoniest dive to the sidewalk he'd ever seen.

He stifled a laugh as he got out of the car. Not that a lot of people didn't relish the opportunity to sue a wealthy attorney. But Melinda Dumas's act was simply too blatant. He knew exactly what she was up to, and he didn't care.

Most men never got a second chance.

He hurried to her side, pushing past a couple of surprised pedestrians.

"Easy, now. Don't move." Pulling his cell phone from his pocket, he folded his Armani suit jacket into a pillow and slipped it beneath Melinda's head. "I'm calling 911. We'll get you an ambulance right away."

"An ambulance?" She looked up at him with eyes that reminded him of brown sugar, except in the courtroom there hadn't been anything sweet about them. She'd been furious with the settlement he'd won from the judge for her ex-husband, Orly Haas. "I don't need—"

"I don't want you to take any chances. Neck injuries can be very serious. We'll get you the best medical treatment possible."

"An ambulance will cost—"

"Don't worry about a thing, Ms. Dumas. I take full responsibility for the accident. I wasn't paying attention, and I ran right into the back of your vehicle. Naturally, I'll cover all the expenses you incur."

Two fine lines furrowed her otherwise flawless forehead. "You know who I am?"

"Yes, I recognized you." She wasn't a woman a man could easily forget.

"And you're not going to argue about who's at fault?"

"Of course not." He adjusted the coat under her head and caught the faint scent of mint. Her shampoo, he suspected. "Are you comfortable?"

"Yes...well, except for my neck."

"I understand." He smothered the smile that threatened and dialed 911.

A small crowd had gathered on the sidewalk, gawkers with nothing better to do with their time. The gambler who'd been up all night was easy to identify from the bags under his eyes, the showgirl en route to rehearsal from her long legs encased in thick socks. Then there was a male tourist in shorts, probably an Easterner, whose legs had been burned a bright red by the high-altitude summer sun.

On the street, drivers maneuvering to get ahead of one another didn't bother to slow, leaving exhaust fumes in their wake.

Paul preferred the scent of mint, which reminded him of a cooling summer drink that would tingle his taste buds while easing the stress of a high-pressure case.

After he finished the 911 call, Melinda glanced at her limo and the man standing next to it. "I really need to get my client to the airport." She started to sit up.

Gently, Paul pressed her down again. "I'll take care of everything. You rest right there until the ambulance comes. I don't want you compounding your injury in any way."

Standing, he signaled a passing cab, then helped get the passenger and his luggage from the limo into the taxi, and paid the fare. By then the ambulance was pulling up, siren blaring, red lights blinking.

Paul hunkered down beside Melinda again. "Are the keys in the limo?"

"Uh, yes. Why?" Her brows tugged together above a slender, straight nose.

"I'll get one of my people to drive it to the repair shop." Although at a glance, he could barely detect a scratch on the bumper. "It's a body shop I've used before, so I know they do good work. Naturally, I'll pay for the expense."

"You're being awfully nice about this, Mr.

DeMarco.'' A hint of both skepticism and surprise laced her words.

''Call me Paul, please. And it's the least I can do after causing the accident.''

''Yes, well...''

The ambulance driver slipped a brace around her neck, then driver and helper lifted her onto a backboard, freeing Paul's pillowed jacket.

Paul picked it up from the sidewalk and shook it out. The jacket would need a trip to the cleaners, but that didn't worry him overly much. He had a housekeeper to take care of those details.

''As soon as I get things arranged here, I'll take my nephews home and come by the hospital to see how you are.''

''Your nephews?'' she gasped. ''Are there children in the car? Were they hurt?''

''They're fine, except for the lecture I'm about to give them for distracting me while I'm driving.''

''I don't want you to punish them. I'm sure they didn't realize they might cause an accident.''

Her concern for the boys reaffirmed Paul's earlier impression that she was an empathetic person and a good mother, who dearly loved her own two kids. Both in the courtroom and at the conference table, her first thought had been for her children's future.

Resting a reassuring hand on her shoulder, he found her deceptively fragile and thoroughly feminine beneath the gabardine chauffeur's jacket. ''I promise I won't draw a drop of their blood.''

The faint hint of a smile curved her full lips. ''Thanks.''

''We gotta move her now, mister,'' the ambulance driver announced.

''I'll see you later,'' Paul promised Melinda, then stepped back out of the way.

With his jacket slung over his shoulder, he watched while the attendants loaded her into the ambulance and the door closed behind her. A quick call to the law student interning at his office for the summer got the ball rolling to transport the limo to the body shop.

Feeling confident, Paul strolled back to the Mercedes. Steven's head was hanging out the window, a sweaty lock of dark brown hair falling across his forehead in much the same way Paul's own hair tended to behave.

''Is the lady gonna die?'' he asked.

''Nope. She'll be fine.'' More than fine, he mused, because he planned to take very good care of her. ''But you're not going to get your ride in a T-6 today, after all.'' The plane was flown by a buddy of his who was an aficionado of the Reno Air Races and in town for a few days. ''I'm going to have to take you guys home to your mom. I've got something important I have to do.''

Both boys groaned in disappointment. ''Aw, Uncle Paul—''

''I'll make it up to you, I promise.'' Whether his nephews knew it or not, their fooling around in the back seat of his car had done him a big favor.

He'd been attracted to Melinda Dumas from the first time he'd met her across the mahogany conference table in his sixth-floor office in downtown Reno, not far from the courthouse. He couldn't do anything about it then. Not while he represented her husband in some rather hostile divorce proceedings.

But that had been a year ago. A lot of water had flowed down the Truckee River since then.

He smiled in anticipation. Nothing in the code of ethics prevented him from pursuing her now. If he could arrange to have her spend a little time in his company, he was confident he could demonstrate he wasn't the ogre she believed him to be.

He was, after all, a responsible guy. Generous to his friends and family members. Good with kids and kind to old ladies. Even charming when the situation demanded it.

Yes, he'd find a way to change Melinda's mind about him, and his motive wasn't to avoid being dragged into court for a trumped-up personal injury suit.

The radiant smile he sensed she was capable of bestowing on a man, plus the zeal and unbeatable spirit that he'd observed in the courtroom, were what inspired him.

STRAPPED DOWN, Melinda couldn't budge. That didn't prevent her from being thrown from side to side and bounced around as the ambulance raced through the streets of Reno. When this was over, she was damn well going to write the mayor about filling the blankety-blank potholes in his fair city.

She'd mention the need for better air-conditioning in ambulances, too. The summer sun had raised the temperature inside the vehicle to that of a baking oven, compounding her vague sensation of motion sickness.

Closing her eyes, she groaned.

Why on earth had Paul DeMarco been so darn nice to her? Those chocolate-brown eyes of his had been filled with concern. Wonderfully sympathetic. He'd admitted guilt. His take-charge attitude told her she had nothing to worry about.

Except this whole neck business was a fake.

A stab of guilt pricked her conscience. She shouldn't have lied to him. For such a tiny fender bender, she shouldn't have even been thinking about suing him.

But he was the man who'd caused her to suffer through one humiliation after another this past year since her divorce from Orly.

Because DeMarco had stuck her with Orly's high-flying gambling debts, she'd had to sell the small home they'd owned in Sparks. Not that it had been all that spectacular a house, but what equity they'd had was now gone.

She'd had to move herself and her children, Nancy and Ryan, in with her brother Zane and become his housekeeper—during those increasingly rare times when he was home. All because she couldn't afford to live on her own. And she'd already sold her shares of the Twin Bar Ranch to her brothers—at Orly's insistence—in order to buy the limo business, which her ex had promised would make them a fortune. Ha!

When school started last fall, Melinda's mother had been the one to buy Nancy and Ryan their new clothes.

And at Christmas, her sister, Kerry, had bought Nancy the fancy skateboard Melinda's daughter had coveted and the bike her son had dreamed of owning.

And her brother Zach had covered the cost of skiing lessons for her children last winter.

To make matters worse, when Melinda finally realized there'd be no presents for the children from Orly, she'd had to race out at the last minute to get something—*anything*—that she could wrap and sign his name to. She desperately didn't want the children to feel unloved by their father, however big a jerk he'd proved himself to be.

With each new humiliation, Melinda had been brought lower and lower. Despite hours of hard work, both driving the limo—which often took her away from her children at night—and trying to round up new business, she couldn't seem to get her head above water.

Because of her sleazebag ex and his shark attorney.

Together, the two men had hurt her children. She'd never forgive them for that.

The ambulance lurched again and ground to a stop at the hospital's emergency entrance.

The opportunity to sue Paul DeMarco was simply the wheels of fate meting out justice at last.

AN HOUR LATER, Melinda was still lying on a gurney in the corridor waiting for X rays, grateful she hadn't suffered a heart attack or some potentially fatal injury. Speed did not appear to be the strong suit for this emergency room.

Of course, her injury was faked, but they didn't know that. Except for a cursory exam by a passing doctor, she'd otherwise been ignored.

Men and women in white jackets or green scrubs hurried past her at frequent intervals, barely glancing in her direction. Periodically, a female voice spoke over a loudspeaker requesting that Dr. Wolfson call extension 36. Based on the repeated page, the doctor was either very popular or ignoring the call.

With Melinda's luck, Wolfson was the doctor who was supposed to take care of her.

Idly, she tried to count the holes in the acoustical ceiling tiles overhead. If something didn't happen soon, she was going to have to get up and go home. She had way too much to do to lollygag around a hospital all day.

"Melinda? Is that you?"

She turned her head at the sound of a woman's voice, no easy matter with the heavy brace on her neck.

"Oh, hi, Leslie. Or since we're in a hospital, should I call you Dr. Hall?"

The attractive, dark-haired woman smiled, her

walnut-brown eyes no longer harboring the wounded look they had when Melinda had first met her.

''Leslie will do just fine. I'm not on duty.''

''Actually, I wish you were. I'm getting tired of lying here with nothing happening.''

Leslie's brows rose with the slightest hint of question.

''Whiplash,'' Melinda explained, trying to ignore the sting of guilt she felt at lying to her future sister-in-law. ''A little fender bender. Nothing serious.'' She forced a smile.

''Soft tissue injuries are no laughing matter. They're hard to diagnose and treat, and the recovery time can be quite lengthy.''

''Well, yeah, I know, but I'm sure I'll get over it in a hurry.'' This was not a conversation she wanted to have. ''So how's it going between you and Zach?''

A slight flush rose to color the doctor's cheeks. ''Just fine, thank you.''

''Have you set the date yet?''

''No, but we're edging ever closer.''

''Good for you. My brother needs a good woman in his life.''

Smiling, Leslie closed her hand over Melinda's. ''And I need a good man in mine.''

That was true enough. Leslie had lost both her husband and son in a tragic accident, but now that she and Zach had fallen in love, her future looked much brighter.

''So how's the mystery of my brother's paternity

coming along?'' Melinda asked. Actually, the question involved both of her brothers, since Zach and Zane were twins. Zach had had his blood tested to see if he could be a donor to Melinda when her arm injury developed complications. The results of the test indicated that Melinda's parents couldn't be the twins' biological parents, which had shocked the entire family.

''Well, you know we've figured out who his biological mother was.''

''Right. Rose Rydic, the singer. I suppose Zach is serenading you in the shower all the time now, showing off.''

The blush deepened again on Leslie's cheeks. ''I think it's safe to assume Zach has found other things to do in the shower besides sing.''

Melinda groaned. ''I don't think I want to hear this.'' She would never be able to think of Zach and Zane as anything but her brothers, despite their lack of a biological connection to her. And their love lives were not something she was eager to discuss.

''Well, Zach keeps searching for clues about his biological father, but so far there isn't much to go on.''

''Maybe Zane will be able to help when he gets home.''

''*If* he gets home,'' Leslie said. ''Zach hasn't heard from him in a while, and he's worried.''

So was Melinda, but she didn't want to admit it out loud. Her brother Zane had slipped into a dark emotional hole following the death of his wife in a tragic car accident that had left Zane unscathed. Since then he hadn't been the same, not even able to find joy in raising the beautiful Arabians he and his wife had lavished so much attention on.

The situation was doubly difficult for Melinda. She and Zane's wife, Jenny, had been best friends in high school. Melinda had introduced the two of them. And then she lost Jen...and in many ways her brother, too. That had been the one small consolation about moving in with Zane at his horse ranch. She had hoped she'd be able to help him.

So far she hadn't done much except cook his meals when he was home and spend her spare time fretting about him. At the moment he was somewhere in South America in search of Arabian breeding stock. Or so he'd said.

Melinda suspected his excuse for the trip was about as lame as her whiplash story.

An orderly arrived at her bedside, one of those men in white who'd traipsed past her a dozen times. "They can take you in the X-ray department now, ma'am."

"About time," she muttered.

Leslie touched her hand one more time. "If you need anything, call me, okay?"

"Will do. Thanks." What she most likely would need was a conscience that no longer worried about little white lies.

Or better yet, no conscience at all when it came to the unscrupulous attorney who had done his best to ruin her children's lives.

CHAPTER TWO

PAUL PACED the waiting area outside the emergency room while others dozed in the hard plastic chairs or stared glassy-eyed at the morning TV soap.

He wasn't generally nervous in his dealings with women, even beautiful women who might intimidate other men. He could flirt when the occasion called for it, make idle chitchat at a cocktail party, invite a woman out on a date as effortlessly as picking up his laundry.

But this was different. *Melinda Dumas* was different.

It wasn't that she was the most beautiful woman in the universe. Reno was full of traditional beauties with long dancer's legs and anorexic bodies. Melinda was more than that....

Halting at the window to look out at the cars in search of a parking space in the hospital lot, he slid his hands into his pockets.

Dependable was the word that came to him. Open and honest. And a natural beauty who didn't need a lot of artifice to hide any tiny flaws.

He doubted she colored her hair. The sun-streaked highlights in among the truffle-colored curls came from being outdoors, probably while riding a horse at the ranch she owned with her brothers.

And on the rare occasions when he'd seen her smile, her sweet brown-sugar eyes sparkled like the sun glistening off Mount Rose, the hill on the outskirts of Reno.

Her voice was clear and feminine, her laughter a warm soprano that fluttered around a room, touching everything as lightly as a butterfly. Despite the stress of the divorce, she'd laughed like that with her kids in the courthouse hallway one morning, and Paul had wanted her to share that laughter with him.

Now that the bitter divorce was behind her, their adversarial relationship past and forgotten—at least as far as he was concerned—he hoped he could get her to laugh like that again.

The door to the emergency room swished open, and Melinda appeared, in a wheelchair pushed by a youthful volunteer wearing a candy-stripe uniform.

With a smile and a sense of relief, Paul stepped forward. He eyed the thick foam-rubber brace that circled Melinda's neck with mixed feelings. Her injury, such as it was, had provided them with a second opportunity to get acquainted, but he didn't kid himself.

A woman who'd fake a whiplash in order to file a lawsuit against him—to get even, he suspected—wouldn't easily fall into his arms. Her expression told him that as she narrowed her eyes with anything but pleasure at seeing him.

That flash of independence, of stubborn pride, was

something he could respect. It made him want to get to know her better. And not as her enemy.

"You're here," she said with little enthusiasm.

"I promised I'd come back for you. I wouldn't want you to have to take a cab home."

"I do run a limo service. I wouldn't have to—"

"But I feel responsible for your injury." And maybe for some part of the residual anger in her eyes. Not that he hadn't simply been doing his job and doing it well when he'd represented her husband. It wasn't his fault that he was far more capable an attorney than the lawyer she'd hired. Ethically, he had to do his best for his clients, even those he didn't personally like. "Please let me do this for you. Take you home, I mean."

"Your nephews?"

"Back safe and sound with their mother, and no worse for wear, I assure you." Of course, the boys had badgered him into promising them a ride in his own Cessna at the earliest opportunity, as well as a swim in his pool—promises he'd willingly granted. More times than not, his house was overrun by his sisters and their children, a situation he didn't mind in the least.

Melinda Dumas exhaled in defeat. "All right, you can drive me home to the ranch. At least I'll be able to make a few calls and maybe stir up some business while the limo's being fixed."

He claimed the volunteer's place behind the wheelchair, dismissing the girl with a smile. "How long did the doctor say your recovery might take?"

''It could be as long as six weeks.''

Perfect. ''You do have someone to take care of you, don't you?'' He pushed Melinda toward the automatic doors. People who'd been waiting in the lobby eyed him with either disinterest or envy.

She lifted her shoulders in a gesture made awkward by the neck brace. ''I'm fine. I can take care of myself.''

''Oh, I can't allow that.'' Halting abruptly, he stepped around in front of her, hunkering down so they were eye to eye. ''I'm sure the doctor doesn't want you to do any heavy lifting, and you'll need to rest. Who's at the ranch?''

''There's Ramón. He's our foreman.''

''He'd make a good nursemaid, would he?''

''If you happen to be a horse with a strained ligament,'' she admitted with a wry smile. ''But really—''

''Then I'm taking you to my house, where you can be properly cared for.'' He stood, the decision made, as far as he was concerned.

''You're what?'' she gasped, her voice climbing half an octave and drawing the attention of those sitting around the waiting room. ''I'm not going to move in with you. I don't care who was at fault in the accident.''

Every head in the waiting room swung in their direction.

Paul ignored the onlookers. ''Why not? I've got a big house with lots of rooms, and a housekeeper who loves to fuss over people. She'll be thrilled to have something more to do than leave a casserole in the oven for me for dinner.''

''I can't...I mean, it's ridiculous to think... What about my children?''

''They can come, too. I've got a pool and a Ping-Pong table. Shuffleboard court. One of those foosball games. And Tilly—'' he grasped the wheelchair handles again and shoved it forward ''—she's my housekeeper. She loves to make pizzas and bake cookies. All my nephews and nieces love to come visit. Your kids will have a great time.''

''I have a business to run. If I lay off for six more weeks, I'll be bankrupt. I can't possibly—''

''Okay, we'll try it for two weeks,'' Paul said, hoping he'd have plenty of time to get to know her by then. ''What do you say? I'll even agree to pay for lost income. After that, you ought to be well enough to manage on your own.''

Sputtering, Melinda twisted around in the chair and looked up at him as best she could, given the limitations of her neck brace. The damn thing itched like crazy already. Wearing it for an hour, much less an entire day, was going to be torture. Six weeks would be impossible.

When no damage to her neck was visible on the X ray, the doctors had taken the safe route, as she'd known they would. A patient complaining of neck problems following an accident was all but guaranteed to be sent home with a brace—wrapped so tightly she already felt like she was being strangled.

''Two weeks?'' she questioned.

"With your income fully insured by me."

How could she refuse his offer? If she were really hurt, his generosity would be a godsend. It wasn't as if he was a stranger or a felon she didn't dare trust. She'd even read in the newspaper that he'd been honored by the local Big Brothers program, one of many community awards he'd won over the years, including recognition as the bar association's Outstanding Citizen last year. As far as Reno movers and shakers were concerned, Paul DeMarco was one of the good guys. A court—or a jury—would expect her to accept his offer. Unless she was lying.

Which she was.

Mentally she began to sweat. She'd really backed herself into a corner this time.

"Is it a deal?" he asked. "Two weeks, and then we'll reevaluate your medical condition."

"Are you always this bossy?"

"Probably." Wheelchair in his grasp, he sailed through the doorway and out into the afternoon heat. The bright sun glared off the white concrete sidewalk, making his eyes crinkle at the corners when he was forced to squint. "It comes from being the oldest of four children."

"Great," she muttered.

"Then I take it we have an agreement."

"Yes, I suppose we do," she said with a defeated sigh. Two weeks, but not a minute longer. She'd think of it as a two week vacation—at Paul DeMarco's expense. She shuddered at the thought.

Totally dumfounded by his arrogance, and his

concern, Melinda knew there was no way she'd be able to tell Paul DeMarco no. Little wonder he was such a successful attorney. Judges and juries must fall at his feet. Or else he walked right over them, whichever was easier, she thought with grudging respect.

He sure as hell had stomped on her lawyer at every turn—metaphorically speaking.

She could have called Kerry to take care of her long enough for Paul to be satisfied with her phony whiplash story, except her sister had set off on some geological exploration in the high desert. Why her siblings had such urges to leave home was beyond Melinda.

Their mother was finding it hard to keep up with the grandkids these days. Besides, Eleanor Dumas didn't like to be gone from her husband for too long, since he'd had a mild heart attack a few years ago. And considering Melinda's parents now lived in an upscale senior citizens' town house community, she couldn't move in with them even temporarily—not with the kids.

No, using her parents as an out wasn't going to work.

Paul wheeled her up to his car, arrogantly parked in a No Parking zone. His reflection in the glossy finish made him look impossibly tall and broad-shouldered, an impressive male of the species by any woman's definition. He'd removed his tie since the accident, and his shirt collar gaped open, revealing an enticing shadow of dark hair at his throat.

Melinda gritted her teeth. Her mother had always told her lying would get her into trouble.

For the past thirty-two years, Melinda had been pretty good about telling the truth. Until now.

Fortunately, there was no way this side of insanity that she would ever fall for the man who had helped her ex take her to the cleaners—no matter how physically appealing that man might be.

PAUL FOLLOWED Melinda's directions to get to the Twin Bar Ranch. Although it wasn't all that far from Reno, there was an increasing sense of remoteness after he left the main highway.

Scrub growth stretched out on either side of the dirt road as he drove up into the foothills. As the altitude rose, the growth changed, became thicker, more lush and green, although nothing like the pine forests that surrounded Lake Tahoe at higher elevations. At the same time, the outside temperature dropped by a couple of degrees.

In his rearview mirror, he could see the desert where Reno had grown helter-skelter, stretching out into the hazy distance. He'd been raised here and knew the area. Flew his own plane above the desert terrain. But he hadn't seen it from quite this perspective before.

"Zane's ranch is right around the next bend," Melinda said.

He glanced at her, feeling sorry for the discomfort the neck brace must be causing her. "Is this where you grew up?"

"No, the main ranch is back behind us, where the road split to the left. Zach lives there now. He's sort of engaged to be engaged."

"Your brother Zane must not like having neighbors too close."

"He and his wife wanted to raise Arabians. When Dad retired and divided the property among us kids, Zane picked this section. There was an old army cavalry post here that he wanted to restore. I think he and his wife, Jenny, did a heck of a job."

As promised, when Paul rounded the next corner, the ranch house and outbuildings came into view. Constructed of native stone and weathered wood, they made an impressive sight. So did the sleek Arabians grazing in a nearby pasture.

"Looks like your brother knew what he was doing," Paul commented.

"Do you know anything about horses?"

"They're big, and somebody needs to follow them with a large scoop."

She rolled her eyes.

"I've ridden a few times, if that's what you're asking. When you're raised on a hundred-by-fifty-foot city lot, there's not a whole lot of room for a horse."

"No, I suppose not."

"We had a dog, though. A basset hound named Derrek. He didn't much like being ridden."

Paul saw her fighting not to laugh, and smiled to himself. He'd break through the barrier between them yet. It was all a question of time and patience.

For a good cause, he had plenty of both.

As he pulled the car to a stop near the house, two youngsters came running out of the horse barn. They slowed when they didn't recognize the car. A tall, wiry man in cowboy boots and hat sauntered out of the barn behind them, his burnished complexion the shade of the desert mountains in which he lived. The foreman, Paul assumed.

"Are you really sure you want my children to move in on you?" Melinda asked. "They can be a handful."

"They'll be fine. I like kids."

"But you don't have any of your own?"

"Nope. Never been married." Not for lack of his sisters' matchmaking efforts, however. Every time he turned around, they were trying to fix him up with one woman or another. Somehow it had never worked out. Nor had the relationships he'd developed on his own. There always seemed to be something lacking—probably a failing of his, he mused. He hadn't been able to imagine spending a lifetime with any of them.

In truth, as a divorce lawyer he knew better than most that marriages failed. Hearts were broken, financial futures destroyed. He didn't ever plan to put himself—or a woman—at that kind of high emotional and fiscal risk. The rest of his family depended upon him too much.

And he remembered all too clearly how devastated his mother had been when his father died. Paul had been equally desolate.

No, he'd leave the marriage business to his siblings and wish them well. But he had no plans to go there himself.

He climbed out of the car, waved to the kids and went around to help Melinda. She was already on her feet before he got there.

"Mommy!" The little girl came running across the yard and threw her arms around Melinda's waist.

The boy was only paces behind his sister.

"What happened to your neck, Mommy?" the girl asked.

"Nothing, really. Well..." Melinda met Paul's dark-eyed gaze over the heads of her children and clamped her mouth shut. The pines, shifting in a light breeze, dappled his face with sunlight, emphasizing his strong jaw and firm mouth. His determination. Explanations were going to be tricky. She didn't want to worry her children, but she couldn't give away her charade, either. "I had a little accident. Nothing serious, honey. And this gentleman was kind enough to drive me home. Say hello to Mr. DeMarco. Paul, these are my children, Nancy and Ryan."

"Hi, kids."

Nancy, her outgoing daughter, smiled brightly, revealing two uneven front teeth. "Hi. I'm eight and I've got two loose teeth. The tooth fairy gave me a whole dollar for the last one I lost."

"Hey, that's great," Paul said.

More cautious, Ryan extended his hand. "Hi."

"Nice to meet you." Paul accepted the handshake

man-to-man. ''Guess what, guys? You and your mom are going to come stay at my place for a while.''

''How come?'' Nancy asked, troubled by the news.

Because my fib has gotten totally out of hand, Melinda mentally groaned.

''So I can help take care of your mom while her neck gets better,'' Paul said.

Melinda opened her mouth to offer a better explanation, but Paul cut her off. ''I've got a pool and a shuffleboard court.''

Nancy's brown eyes brightened. ''Really?''

''My grandma plays shuffleboard,'' Ryan said solemnly. ''She taught me how to play, too.''

''Then I'll bet you'll be able to beat me,'' Paul said. ''I always hit the puck too hard.''

''It's called a disk,'' Ryan informed him.

Melinda slid her hand around the back of Ryan's head and tugged him closer to her. Such a serious child and so dear to her heart. He sorely needed a father to boost his self-confidence. Orly had never had the time or inclination.

''With all this talk of your pool and shuffleboard court, I get the distinct impression you're trying to coax my children into pressuring me,'' she told Paul.

His smile was not in the least repentant. ''Part of my job is to be persuasive.''

Indeed it was, and he did it very well—in a courtroom or out. Her children had that hopeful look in their eyes, a spark of eagerness. They'd been bored on the ranch since school let out, too far from their friends for easy play dates. And Ramón, as good as he was with horses, wasn't a whole lot of fun as a playmate for six- and eight-year-olds. But he was the best and most reliable baby-sitter she had available with her unpredictable work schedule.

She waved her foreman over. "Ramón, this is Paul DeMarco. The children and I will be staying for a few days at his house. I'll leave you the phone number in case you need me for anything." She was too embarrassed to call her mother or brother—they'd never approve of her scheme.

Without changing his usual stoic expression, he slid a critical glance at Paul, measuring the man she was about to go off with. "Me and the horses will be fine, Miss Melinda."

"Zane might try to reach me."

"I'll let him know where you are."

"Yes, well..." So much for getting your foreman's ringing approval. "All right, children. If we're going to go stay with Mr. DeMarco for a few days, we'll have to pack our suitcases."

The youngsters cheered and went running into the house, Nancy in the lead.

Melinda followed them up the steps to the wide veranda, then stopped to look back at Paul, who was right behind her. "Do you always get your way?"

His dark eyes skimmed over her, seeing right through her chauffeur's uniform, it seemed, bringing a flush to her skin and an awareness to her midsection she didn't want to acknowledge. Wasn't going to acknowledge, she reminded herself. How could she even consider such a reaction to Paul DeMarco? No doubt it was her lie that was making her feel anxious.

"Usually." He nodded. "When I set my mind to something."

Whirling, she snapped open the screen door and stalked inside.

Amused, Paul followed her. He rather liked a woman with a temper, liked the way her eyes flashed a don't-mess-with-me warning. A cloyingly sweet woman made him nervous after a while. Bored him.

He didn't imagine Melinda would ever bore him.

The living room was darker than he'd expected, with heavy, overstuffed chairs, hardwood floors and a big rock fireplace with few personal touches. When he thought of Melinda he imagined bright colors—reds and fiery oranges. Or in her quiet moments, if she had any, there would be pastels—pinks and blues and soft yellows. Feminine colors. And the sweet scent of mint shampoo.

This room, he realized, belonged to her brother.

For the next few weeks, Paul intended to discover Melinda's favorite color along with myriad other facets of her personality.

"You can wait here while I pack," she told him as she headed toward a doorway leading to the bedroom wing of the house.

"I'll come help," he said mildly. "You don't want to overdo or you might reinjure your neck."

MELINDA GRIMACED. This was not a good plan.

Paul had practically tied her in the chair in her bedroom while he did the packing. *Rest,* he'd insisted. *Relax,* he'd said.

Oh, sure, as if she could while he was rummaging through her underwear drawer.

He held up a lacy number in a flesh tone. "Nice. Do you wear these under your uniform?"

"Could you just get on with the packing? I have to be sure the children have what they need, too."

With a smug smile, he dropped the undies into the open suitcase on the bed. That pair was followed by one in baby blue and another in black. He *would* have to discover her one indulgence. She liked the feel of silk against her skin. It was no big deal.

Except when the silk slid through his long, tapered fingers, she felt it as an intimate caress, and her breathing turned shallow.

She shoved herself up from the chair and winced. "I can take it from here."

In a quick movement, he reached out to steady her. "No, you can't. You hurt your neck just getting up."

"I hurt my *arm,* not my neck," she protested.

"Your arm?"

He was the most exasperating, most attentive man. And far too unsettling when he touched her. "I broke my arm a few weeks ago and just got it out of the cast yesterday. It's a little tender, is all." Worse than that, actually, but she had no intention of admitting it ached liked crazy whenever she moved it. Or even when she didn't.

"All the more reason why you need to let me take care of things for you."

"Mr. DeMarco—"

"Paul."

"—I don't want you handling my undies. Okay?"

He slowly arched a dark brow. "I don't recall any other women complaining about my technique."

If she'd had two good arms, she would have cold-cocked him. With two older brothers, she'd learned how to do that. But not when a sudden surge of heat raced through her body and zeroed in on her nether regions.

Good grief! She couldn't remember any other man having that effect on her. And she didn't want Paul to be the one now but her body kept betraying her good reason.

She gritted her teeth. "I want you to leave my things alone. Now! Wait for us in the living room. Or outside. But *not* in my bedroom. I'm going to see to the children and finish my *own* packing later." With that, she whirled and stalked down the hallway toward the kids' bedroom.

Behind her, she heard the low rumble of Paul's laughter. It skittered along her spine, burrowing into that same spot where the heat of his remark had already blazed a path.

She marched into the bedroom to discover the twin beds and the floor in between strewn with the children's belongings.

"Kids, we're not moving to Mr. DeMarco's house. We're just going to stay a couple of days." A visit as short as Melinda could make it and still justify the lawsuit she had planned. She'd promised two weeks. With luck, she could get out of there sooner. "You don't have to take everything you own."

"I want to take my Lego," Ryan insisted, struggling to lift a plastic stacking box overflowing with pieces of the building toy. "He might not have any toys to play with."

"How 'bout just *some* of your Lego?" Melinda suggested, in search of a compromise.

"Is Mr. DeMarco your boyfriend?" Nancy asked. Her bed was covered with clothes, her nail polishing kit, which had long since run out of red, and a jar of beads for making necklaces.

Melinda put the jar back on the bookcase next to Nancy's bed. "No, he's definitely not my boyfriend. He's just—" *Interfering in my life. Again.* "—helping out because of the accident."

"He's cool-looking. Sort of like a movie star." Nancy stuffed three pairs of jeans into her suitcase none too neatly and reached for her bead jar again.

Handsome or not, Paul was way too slick for Melinda's taste.

"*I'm* supposed to be the man of the house when Daddy's not around," Ryan said. "He told me so."

"And you still are, sweetie." Giving her son a quick hug, Melinda pulled a few pairs of briefs from his dresser drawer, something he was likely to overlook in his determination to take extra toys along. "But it's okay for you to be a little boy, too. Mommy doesn't want you to grow up too fast."

Trying to get tops and bottoms that more or less matched, Melinda helped the children finish packing. Then she organized her own clothes and personal items.

A half hour later, she'd changed into slacks and a cotton blouse, and they were all in Paul's Mercedes heading back toward town. She'd given Ramón Paul's phone number in case anyone called. Both her neck and arm were beginning to ache, and her teeth were numb from clamping her jaw so hard.

How on earth was her play-acting, forget her peace of mind, going to survive so much as one day under the same roof with Paul? Much less two weeks! Lord, why had she ever agreed to such an arrangement? Even now he was regaling the children with stories about his youth. Suckering them into his life.

He told them about the time he'd broken his arm jumping into the Truckee River at a spot where it was only two inches deep.

Then there was the Sunday morning when he was four and he'd picked up all the newspapers from the neighbors' driveways in his little red wagon, proudly delivering them to his own house. The police had arrived at his front door, much to the chagrin of his late-sleeping parents.

He described the bow and arrow he'd made out of willow, and the arrow he'd impaled in the side of a laundry truck, confident in his own mind that he was an Indian brave protecting his village.

While Melinda fought to keep a straight face, her children betrayed her with their giggles. She didn't want them to like Paul so easily, not when she was determined—on their behalf—to gain her revenge by suing him.

She didn't want to like him at all. But that possibility became increasingly remote with each minute she spent in his company. Not a good thing.

She'd set up this lie. She had to live with it or she'd never get her revenge. But you couldn't exactly take a man who made your children laugh to court, could you? A man who made your own heart ache with a dreadful sense of loneliness—which she damn well was going to ignore.

They reached the upscale residential area southeast of town and drove on curving roads past homes that cost at least a half-million dollars. He pulled into the driveway of a dune-colored two-story house with natural high-desert landscaping of decorative rocks and drought-resistant pine trees.

A gardener using a blower to rake the pine needles away from the white-stone ground covering waved in their direction.

Paul returned the wave before switching off the car ignition. "What do you think of the house?" he asked her.

She gazed at the place through the windshield, her emotions vacillating between envy and anger. "How big a piece of this did Orly's legal fees pay for?"

He chuckled. "None. I had another client who had to liquidate before his wife took him to the cleaners. He sold it to me for a song."

She shifted on the seat and leveled him a look. "You mean you cheated his wife out of her rightful share of the community property."

"No. That's not precisely what happened. It was business...." He had the good sense to flush before opening the car door to get out. "Come on, kids. Let's check out the pool."

Melinda leaned her head back against the seat. Despite Paul's obvious charm and his incredible sex appeal, she needed to remember he was a first-degree shark. She hadn't been the only woman to suffer at his hands financially. And if she'd learned anything about the law and attorneys in the past couple of years, she wouldn't be the last.

IN AN UPSTAIRS BEDROOM, Melinda stood by a big picture window overlooking a kidney-shaped pool glistening turquoise in the afternoon sunshine. In the distance, Mount Rose stretched up from the valley floor like a dusky cone. Beyond that, the eastern slope of the Sierras soared to impressive heights.

Everything about Paul DeMarco, including his house and its view, was impressive. Too much so, Melinda thought.

She turned back to Tilly Boudine, Paul's housekeeper, who was busily unpacking Melinda's bag. Short and stout, the woman reminded Melinda of a top that kept on spinning and spinning. Despite her age, which Melinda guessed to be somewhere between sixty and seventy, Tilly did not appear to have the word *slow* as part of her vocabulary.

''I wish you'd let me do that,'' Melinda said.

''Nonsense. Mr. D said you were to rest, and that's just what you'll do while you're here. I'll see to that.'' Pulling open a drawer in the cherry-wood dresser, Tilly neatly slipped Melinda's nightgown inside.

''Does Mr. DeMarco often bring women home for R and R?'' The room was decidedly feminine, with a rose comforter on the queen-size bed and frilly shades on the two lamps, as if prepared for female visitors.

On the run, Tilly snapped out a pair of Melinda's jeans and headed for the closet. ''Sakes, no. Now, he's brought a lady friend by a time or two for a swim, I'll give you that. And maybe a cozy dinner. You know how it is with men.'' Efficiently, she hung the pants on a hanger, straightened them just so, then retrieved a pair of shorts from the suitcase.

''Of course, I don't know exactly what happens after they have supper,'' Tilly admitted. ''I mind my own business. Got my own little place downstairs, out of the way. Everything I need. My own TV. He buys me cable so I can watch the shopping channel. And I've got a nice city view. It's real pretty during the Christmas season with all the lights, you know?''

''I'm sure it is,'' Melinda agreed when the housekeeper managed to take a breath before returning to the suitcase once again.

"Can't think when Mr. D has ever had the same woman over to visit twice. Can't seem to settle, I'd say. His sisters fret about that, but I'm not worried. He'll settle when he's ready. Most men do."

A committed bachelor, Melinda decided. That was just fine with her.

By now her head was beginning to ache from watching Tilly race back and forth across the room. It was like following a tennis match with a big, round, happy ball.

Surrendering any effort to help, Melinda sat down on an upholstered lounging chair, the floral fabric in bright shades of rose and green. Undoing her neck brace, she set it aside and leaned back, relaxing. It was all too possible she could learn to enjoy being taken care of.

"I'll just put your makeup and things in the bathroom," Tilly announced. "We always have plenty of hot water and there's a nice big whirlpool tub to relax in when you're tired. Of course, it's the very devil to clean, what with the bending over and all." She vanished into a room with desert-beige tile and bright lights. "I'll have to find you some fresh towels. Be back in a minute," she called over her shoulder.

While Melinda was idly gazing into the bathroom, contemplating the uses of a Jacuzzilike bathtub in ways she shouldn't be considering, the door on the opposite side opened. She gasped at the sight of Paul standing in the doorway—lean, powerful and wearing nothing but tight-fitting swim trunks that cupped him like a woman's hand.

He strolled across the bathroom pretty as you please. Brazen. Self-confident. Melinda couldn't help eyeing the intriguing swirls of dark hair across his chest, the heavy gold chain circling his neck.

"Is Tilly getting you settled in?"

Cursing her own weakness, she swallowed hard. "Yes, thank you."

"The kids wanted to take a swim. I told 'em to put on their suits. I hope it's okay."

Nodding, she licked her lips. "Fine. Is that your, uh, bedroom on the other side of the—"

"Oh, yeah, sorry about that. We have to share the bathroom, unless you want to go down the hall to the guest one. Hope that's not a problem."

"No. No. Of course not." She swallowed again and tried to make a joke of the arrangement. "Unless there isn't a lock on the door."

His lips slid into a wickedly sexy grin. "Funny about that. The original owner didn't believe in a little thing like a lock coming between him and his wife. She was the one who decorated this room, by the way." He shrugged. "Of course, like most married couples, they ended up divorced."

Melinda closed her eyes and pictured herself shoving the queen-size bed up against the door. The dresser, too.

"You don't have to worry, Melinda." His voice was low and soft. Intimate. And very close to her.

"I'm an honorable man and wouldn't think of coming into a woman's bedroom without an invitation."

Opening her eyes, she found him crouched down in front of her, his face only inches from hers. His eyes were a devilish shade of black, almost the same color as his dark hair. His lips were full and tempting.

She swallowed back a sigh. What she needed was a locksmith who made emergency calls.

Still crouching beside her, he reached past her to the end table and picked up the neck brace she'd left there.

"You don't want to forget to wear this." With incredible gentleness, he looped the brace around her neck and fastened the velco tabs, then lifted her hair out of the way.

The gesture raised gooseflesh on her arms and sent heat spreading through her midsection.

"I want you to get well as quickly as possible."

On second thought, a locksmith wasn't going to solve her problems. Getting the heck out of here would be a better plan.

But she'd promised. Made an agreement. *Two weeks.*

As a rule, when she gave her word it was like money in the bank—assuming she *had* any money. In this case, she didn't dare break her vow for fear that somewhere downstream, Paul—and a jury of her peers—would hold it against her.

They'd know this whole whiplash business was a scam. And they'd be right.

But if she was going to stick it out for two weeks, it would be so much better if Paul kept his distance. And if her heart would stop its erratic beating, much like one of her limos' cylinders gone bad.

CHAPTER THREE

LAUGHTER DRIFTED UP from the pool, drawing Melinda to the window. Tilly had finished fussing over her and doing the unpacking, leaving Melinda alone—with her itchy neck brace.

''Marco!'' Paul called, his eyes tightly closed as he stood in the shallow end of the pool.

''Polo!'' the children chorused in response, both of them clinging to the edge on opposite sides of the pool.

Paul made a splashing dive for Ryan, missing him by a foot or so, which sent the boy into gales of infectious giggles.

Melinda's heart squeezed tight. What irony that the man with whom she was trying to even the score was the same one who could so easily bring her little boy out of his shell.

Paul also had the potential to hurt her son by allowing Ryan to care for him too much, and then abandoning him, as Orly had effectively done.

Or, she thought with a new stab of guilt, she could be the one to hurt her son if she allowed him to become too close to Paul. The suit she was planning didn't bode well for long-term relationships between Paul and any member of her family, herself included.

Despite all that, she noted how Paul moved with athletic grace through the water, slipping beneath the surface to become an indistinct shadow, then rising again like Neptune, water streaming from his dark hair and broad shoulders. Everything about him spoke of confidence. Wealth. And dynamic masculinity.

Closing her eyes, she tried to focus only on the man's wealth, which he earned by forcing women and children into poverty, all for the sake of his *male* clients. But the image of his bare, well-muscled chest and the sound of his rich laughter made it difficult to concentrate on anything other than his virility.

She'd been celibate for too damn long.

With a sigh, she turned away from the window. She had a business to run and bills to pay. Paul might be free to spend an afternoon in the sun, but she wasn't. Not entirely.

Using the phone on the nightstand, she punched in the number of Natalie Greene, her former neighbor, who drove Advanced Limo's second vehicle for a little extra pin money.

''Hi, Natalie, how are things going?'' Melinda asked when her friend answered the phone.

''The usual complaints—a husband who doesn't appreciate me, not enough money, kids who refer to me as slave-mom.'' She laughed, and Melinda pictured her friend's bright blue eyes sparkling with a humor that couldn't be repressed no matter how many battles she got into with her beer-drinking husband. ''How 'bout you, Mel?''

"I, uh, had a little fender bender this morning. Looks like I'll be out of business for a couple of days."

"Are you hurt?"

"No. No, not really." She bit her lip, hoping her call wasn't being taped—not that she was innately suspicious of her host. "But Wally's going to be in the shop for a couple of days." For reasons she couldn't explain, she'd named the company's limos Wallowing Wally and Limping Larry. Wally was the one she usually drove. Limping Larry, with its irritable carburetor, was Natalie's regular ride. "You'll have to handle whatever calls we get."

"Sure, I can do that. I'm already scheduled to handle the Metcalfs' fiftieth anniversary affair tonight."

"Right."

"Tomorrow morning might be a problem, though, if we get a run to the airport or something."

Melinda swung her legs up onto the bed and leaned back against the stacked pillows. True luxury. "How come? Something with the kids?"

"No. I made an appointment for me and Rocky to see a marriage counselor." Natalie and her husband had been having problems off and on for years, among them Rocky's habit of downing too many beers at the local pub almost every evening after work. Lately, she'd suspected that infidelity had been added to the list of stresses in their marriage.

"Well, that's good, isn't it?" Melinda asked. "If he'll go, I mean."

"Yeah. If he'll go." Natalie didn't sound optimistic.

"I'll keep my fingers crossed for you. Meanwhile, is it okay if I forward the limo calls to your phone—let you handle them? If you have a conflict, you can give Martin Smelling a shout to fill in." Martin was a reliable college student who worked as an extra driver when Melinda or Natalie was overbooked.

"Sure, fine by me."

"If you have any questions, you can reach me at..." She checked the sticker on the phone and read off the numbers.

"You're not at the ranch?"

"No, I'm, uh, the kids and I are staying with a, uh, friend for a couple of days."

Melinda could practically see Natalie's blond eyebrows shoot up an inch. "A friend? Is there something you'd like to tell me, Mel?"

"There's nothing to tell. We won't be staying here long." Melinda would leave now if it wouldn't put the kibosh on the suit she had planned. And if the kids hadn't been having such a good time. And if Paul wasn't being so darn nice.

She glanced toward the window as a new wave of laughter rippled upward from the pool. "Look, hon, I gotta go. Call me if there's a problem."

Fending off Natalie's questions, Melinda managed to extricate herself from the phone conversation without revealing exactly with whom she was staying or why. She had a sudden urge to be downstairs, part of the fun, to enjoy all the laughter firsthand.

Her children's giggles combined with Paul's deeper chuckle were a temptation she couldn't ignore a moment longer.

If nothing else, she had to protect Nancy and Ryan from being hurt by a man who didn't have their best interests at heart.

PAUL TAPPED THE FOOSBALL right down the center of the tabletop. His opponents spun their paddles frantically, missing the ball entirely, and it slid into their goal.

"Oh, man, you scored again!" Ryan complained, but with little ill will.

"You've got to slide that stick back and forth so you can hit the ball," Paul explained.

"I'm too little."

"No, you're not, Ryan." Nancy grinned up at Paul, her features a dainty heart-shaped replica of her mother's. "He's too big and fast, and he's been practicing. We'll get better if we just keep trying."

"In a few days I won't be able to score on you at all," Paul assured the children.

Melinda's kids were terrific. Bright and alert; good sports, too. Despite the divorce, Orly and Melinda appeared to be raising their youngsters with a minimum of trauma. It made Paul proud that he'd fought for Orly's visitation rights, which Melinda had argued fiercely against, he recalled. He'd been surprised by her attitude toward her children's father, but a man had a right to see his kids. The children needed their dad.

Paul remembered all too well the trauma of losing his father. Even though he'd been fifteen—practically an adult—the burden of trying to carry on without his dad had been almost more than he could handle. He'd vowed at his father's graveside that he'd never marry, never have kids, because he wouldn't want children or a wife to be so torn apart inside if he should die.

Between that life-altering experience and the disastrous view of marriage he faced every day as an attorney, he'd decided to leave marriage to the rest of the world. He'd go it on his own. It wasn't as though he didn't have plenty of people in his life to love—his siblings and a covey of nephews and a niece. That should be enough for any man.

Tugging on Paul's shirt, Ryan said, "Could you let us score just once to see how it feels?"

He gave the boy an exaggerated frown. "You don't want me to cheat, do you?"

Solemnly, the boy nodded. "It'd be okay this once."

Paul laughed and told them to set up the ball again. Operating all four sticks on his side of the table, he twirled the paddles. "Okay, kids, give me your best shot."

Nancy lined up the ball and whacked it.

Just as she did, something caught Paul's attention out of the corner of his eye. He glanced toward the sliding glass door into the house, and his hands froze.

Melinda stood there, smiling at her children, looking more than terrific in shorts and a tank top. Her legs were long, tan and smoothly muscled, probably a result of her riding horseback regularly. Above her nicely flared hips, her waist narrowed. His gaze traveled upward to the attractive curve of her breasts, lingering momentarily, and then past the ugly neck brace to her face. Their eyes met, and he felt a bolt of something seriously resembling lust.

"We scored!" Ryan shouted.

"Yay for our team!" Nancy added.

Paul looked down as the ball clattered into his goal. He chuckled. Served him right for being distracted by a woman. A beautiful, *sexy* woman.

Nancy followed his gaze back to Melinda. "Mom, look at all the stuff Paul's got!"

Melinda raised her brows. "Don't you think you should call him *Mr.* DeMarco?"

"But he said—"

"Paul's easier," he told her. "I asked them to call me that."

She eyed him skeptically, then shifted her attention back to her children. "I don't want you taking advantage of Mr. DeMarco's hospitality."

"We're not," Ryan said. "He beats us all the time."

"Does he?"

"Come on, Mom. Let's make it girls against the boys. You play, too."

Studying the foosball table, she shook her head. "I don't know..."

Suppressing a smile at her hesitation, Paul said,

''I wouldn't want you to injure your neck. It's a pretty wild game the way your kids play.''

He could see her spine stiffen, her shoulders straighten and her jaw lock. She was no sweet miss but one hell of a competitor. A man should be wary of a woman like that. If he wasn't careful, he could get an important part of his anatomy handed to him on a platter.

''Thanks for your concern,'' she said, ''but I think I can handle it.''

He imagined she could, given her neck injury was a scam.

A minute later, Paul realized he'd underestimated Melinda by thinking she was merely competitive. She was a *tiger* with those paddles, whirling and spinning them, sliding them back and forth with a vengeance. It was all he could do to keep up.

Nancy cheered when the girls scored first. He and Ryan groaned. Melinda simply looked intense. Paul was glad she wasn't an attorney he had to face across a courtroom. She wasn't someone who gave up easily.

Neither was he. And her determination, her downright stubbornness, fueled the attraction he'd felt for her a year ago. She'd be a formidable opponent.

Or an even more formidable partner—in bed or out.

MELINDA FELT like a country bumpkin who'd crashed a state dinner at the governor's mansion.

"I wish you'd let me help," she told Tilly. "I'm not used to being waited on."

"Nonsense." The housekeeper carried a plate of fried chicken, a bowl of mashed potatoes and a tall pepper grinder from the kitchen into the dining room. "Mr. D wants you to rest and get well, don't you, Mr. D?"

"That's the plan," Paul agreed, smiling. He sat at the head of the white-oak table, which was inlaid with an intricate pattern of yellow birch. Although it was still sunny outside, slender tapers in a desert-rose candelabra glowed with tiny golden flames.

Melinda sat at the foot of the table, her children on opposite sides, faces sunburned, eyes alight with interest and excitement. Tiny heat waves rippled upward from the candles, making her view of Paul shimmer.

"It does Mr. D good to sit down to a proper meal now and then instead of eating in the kitchen all by himself." Tilly bustled back toward the kitchen. "That's not good for his digestion, is what I say."

Nancy whispered, "She sure does talk a lot, doesn't she?"

Placing her finger to her lips, Melinda shushed her daughter.

Paul lifted his shoulders in a shrug. "She was part of the deal when I bought the house. She'd lived here for years and didn't have anywhere else to go when the family broke up."

He made it sound as though having a housekeeper was an altruistic venture for him. In Melinda's case, *she* was the housekeeper at her brother's house. Her own, too, when she'd had a house. Which she didn't now, thanks to you-know-who.

"Did you know Paul has a boat?" Nancy asked.

"The family likes to water-ski at Pyramid Lake," he explained.

Tilly bustled in again, this time with a huge bowl of salad. "There's homemade brownies for dessert when you're ready."

"You're going to spoil us," Melinda said as the woman hurried back into the kitchen.

"He's got a plane, too, Mom." Carefully, Ryan selected a drumstick from the platter of chicken and placed it on his fine china plate—a marked contrast to their durable ceramic dishes at the ranch. "He says he'll take us flying and stuff."

"A plane?" Melinda questioned.

"A twin-engine Cessna 310. I frequently have business in Las Vegas and sometimes in San Francisco. It's easier to fly myself rather than deal with airline schedules."

"Sounds to me like you're trying to win the game by being the boy with all the toys."

A grin creased his cheek. "I've got a Harley, too."

She rolled her eyes. He certainly didn't deny himself anything. Then again, a man with as much money as Paul had didn't have to choose between buying his child a bike or paying for the weekly groceries.

All the more reason why she was out of her mind

to even *think* about how attractive he was. In her view, his wealth was based on ill-gotten gains.

As dinner progressed, Paul engaged Nancy and Ryan in a conversation about their school, what classes they enjoyed, if they liked to ride horses. For a bachelor, he was amazingly at ease with children, treating them as though he really cared about their interests and activities.

Despite Orly's hail-fellow-well-met personality, he'd never been as attentive to his own children as Paul had been all afternoon.

Why? she wondered. Why would Paul, her adversary, take such an interest in her children? Or be so concerned about her whiplash injury?

Could he have guessed what she was up to and be planning his own revenge?

AFTER DINNER, Melinda allowed the children to watch one show on the Disney Channel—a special treat for them in a day marked by tons of wondrous experiences at Paul's house—then went upstairs to help them get ready for bed.

Ryan's little fingers worked with care to button his pajama top. "This is a neat house, isn't it, Mom?"

"It's very nice, dear."

"I wish we had a swimming pool."

"Uncle Zane has horses. It's hard to have both."

"Maybe if we asked Uncle Zane, he'd get one," Nancy suggested.

"I don't think so." Melinda tugged her daughter's

nightgown down, straightening it over her slender body. ''I don't want you children to get too used to Paul's pool or this house. Remember, we're not staying here long.'' At this point, she wasn't sure how she'd manage to stay two days, much less the two weeks she'd promised. A prison sentence would have been easier to handle. *Foolish woman.*

Nancy scooted away from her and grabbed a band for her hair. ''We could stay here if he was your boyfriend.''

''Well, he's not. And don't get any ideas about trying to play matchmaker. It won't work.'' Melinda was completely mystified as to where Nancy got all these romantic notions. Bored at the ranch with no one to play with, she'd probably been sneaking too many looks at afternoon soap operas. ''Now into bed, the both of you.''

Ryan yawned hugely and Nancy couldn't stop herself, either.

Melinda tucked them in and kissed them goodnight, her chest tightening with maternal love.

''Sleep tight,'' she whispered as she left the room.

For herself, she didn't expect to sleep well at all. She'd been far too unsettled by the day's events *and* Paul DeMarco.

DOWNSTAIRS, Paul arranged everything for Melinda in the family room while she was putting the kids to bed. He planned a quiet evening, a chance for them to get acquainted.

A chance for her to relax and not be so wary of him.

He fluffed a pillow, placing it on the upholstered chaise longue by the sliding glass door that looked out onto the pool deck. He smiled when he heard her return from upstairs.

''Come on in,'' he said. ''Are the kids okay?''

''They're fine. Worn out by a day in the sun and all the time they logged underwater. I suspect they'll be asleep within minutes.'' She hesitated in the doorway. For dinner, she'd put on jeans instead of shorts, and was wearing a tailored white shirt unbuttoned over her tank top. ''That's a very nice room you've given them.''

''They could have had separate rooms if they'd wanted. It's a big house, but that's the one they picked.''

''They've gotten used to sleeping in twin beds at the ranch. With all the changes they've experienced in the past year, I think it's reassuring for them to be together.''

''As long as they're happy.'' He gestured to the chaise longue. ''Here, come relax awhile. I've got us all set up.''

''Set up?'' She tried to cock her head but the neck brace didn't give her enough flexibility. ''I just wanted to tell you good-night. Thank you for—''

''It's early yet. You've had a long day.'' Crossing the room, he took her arm and led her to the chaise. ''There's nothing on TV except reruns, so I thought I'd read to you while you rested your neck.''

She halted in midstride. "Read?"

"I've got a pretty extensive library." Bookcases crammed with both hardcover books and paperbacks lined two walls in the room. "What's your pleasure—adventure, mystery, biography, legal thrillers? I don't have much to offer in the way of romance, I'm afraid." Although if she were interested in something other than reading material along those lines, he'd be happy to accommodate her.

But he didn't want to rush her.

She tensed as he urged her to be seated, then lifted her feet so she could stretch out. She had great ankles, he noted. Slender. The color of ivory and as smooth as porcelain.

"Romance hasn't been high on my wish list for the past couple of years. Finding a knight in shining armor seems pretty far-fetched after my experience with Orly."

"One bad experience doesn't mean you won't ever be in another relationship."

She narrowed her eyes, drawing her light brown brows together. "We're talking about *reading* romance, right?"

"Of course," he said smoothly, pulling up a chair beside her. Since he'd run into her that morning, he'd been thinking of a bit more action than the printed page allowed. "If you don't have a preference, I picked up a new Paul Bishop police procedural the other day. His books usually read pretty fast."

"That would be fine."

''Great. Just lean back—is that pillow comfortable for you?''

''Perfect.''

''Your neck doesn't hurt too much?'' he asked mildly.

''No, no. It's fine.''

He suspected she'd prefer to yank off the brace and really get comfortable. But if he suggested the idea, it would give away the fact that he knew her injury was phony. He didn't want to do that. Not yet. ''Have I mentioned I think your kids are terrific?''

She smiled slightly. ''I think they're pretty neat.''

''My nephews and niece are good kids, too. You'll have a chance to meet them, I'm sure.'' He sat down in the chair opposite her. ''Do you have any nieces or nephews?''

''Twin nephews. They're Zach's boys, but up until recently they lived with his ex-wife in Las Vegas, so we didn't get to see them very often.''

''Twins run in your family, huh?''

''We thought so until recently, then discovered that wasn't quite true. Turns out Zach and Zane aren't my biological brothers.''

Paul looked at her in surprise. ''They're adopted?''

''It's a little complicated.'' She scooted up a bit on the lounge. ''My mother had a miscarriage and then a stillborn baby before the twins were born. When she went into labor with her third pregnancy, I guess things weren't going well. She was heavily sedated and actually gave birth to a stillborn baby boy.''

Paul shook his head. ''Now I'm really confused. The twins—''

''Another woman at the clinic was in labor at the same time, and she was in even more distress. She died after giving birth to twin boys. The doctor, who was a family friend of my parents, knew that woman had no other family. She wasn't married. I think he must have felt terribly guilty about my mother losing another baby, so when she woke up, she was holding twins in her arms.''

''Good God! The doctor switched the babies! Your parents could have sued—''

''Hardly! My folks were tickled pink.''

Though Paul wasn't an expert in medical malpractice suits, he knew the legal ramifications of switching babies were enormous. ''So they knew what the doctor had done?''

''Not at all. At least, not until a month or so ago, when we learned the twins don't have the same blood type that my parents do.''

''Surely your mother knew when she went into labor that she wasn't pregnant with twins.''

''Well, remember, thirty-eight years ago they didn't have things like sonograms, so twins were sometimes a surprise. And frankly, I don't think Mom wanted to ask too many questions. She was simply too happy to finally have a baby—or babies—in her arms. Dad, too, for that matter.''

"That's an amazing story." Paul was glad he didn't have to defend the doctor's actions in court.

"The story's probably not over yet, either. Zach discovered who his biological mother is, or was. But he's still trying to figure out his father's identity."

"And Zane? What does he think about all this?"

"He's been out of the country for months, so he doesn't know yet."

"Wow! That ought to be quite a shocker when he gets home." Paul picked up the paperback he'd laid on the coffee table, changing the subject with his next comment. "Guess your kids feel really lucky to be living on a horse ranch."

"Not exactly."

"They don't like to ride?"

"They love to ride, but not every day, all day. The ranch is so far away from their friends they never get to see them unless I drop them off somewhere going to or from a limo pickup. Occasionally another mother will bring her child for a visit, but it's really out of the way."

"I suppose that's one of the disadvantages of living on a horse ranch."

"You learn to do the best you can with what you've got."

A trace of bitterness laced her words, which Paul didn't understand. The Twin Bar Ranch was in a beautiful setting, the home he'd seen was modern and had the same conveniences he had right here in the city, with the exception of a pool. But the truth was, not many people in the Reno area had pools.

The winters were too cold, and the boating and waterskiing favored by the locals in the summer generally involved bigger bodies of water.

He glanced down at the book he held and began to read, at the same time wondering why Melinda was so upset about living on a ranch she owned.

MELINDA RIPPED OFF her neck brace the moment she reached her bedroom, then quickly undressed.

Thank God Paul hadn't been reading a romance novel!

His voice was so deep, so sexy, so tempting, that if he'd read a love scene, she would have come totally unglued and pounced on the poor man, probably scaring him to death in the process.

Lord, she couldn't imagine being on a jury listening to him for days—or weeks—and voting for any verdict except the one he wanted. A woman would have to be made of ice to resist him.

Resist his *legal* arguments, she mentally corrected. *If* she were on a jury.

Not the man himself. A woman didn't have to fall for a conniving attorney—no matter how sexy his voice—who stole the financial underpinnings from her. Melinda had more sense than that.

At the sound of someone in the adjoining bathroom, she glanced in that direction and remembered there was no lock on the door. She also recalled the huge whirlpool tub. Big enough for two to enjoy the relaxing water jets together. Except if she and Paul were in the Jacuzzi together, relaxation wouldn't be on her mind. Or his, she imagined.

In a moment of panic, she grabbed her nightgown and slid under the covers. Paul wouldn't come into her room uninvited. He'd said as much. And he wouldn't invite her to share the tub.

Then why did an irritating voice in her head suggest she was glad there was no lock on *either* side of the door?

CHAPTER FOUR

DAWN STAINED Mount Rose a golden hue as Melinda quietly slipped into the pool.

She hadn't slept well. A new bed, unfamiliar night sounds—and a handsome man in the next room—could make a woman restless. A few easy laps would relax her.

Stroking toward the deep end, she breathed rhythmically. The exercise would be good for her aching arm, too; the muscles still weren't recovered from six weeks in a cast. The pool had looked so tempting yesterday, but she'd been reluctant to don her ancient two-piece swimsuit with Paul around. With luck, she'd be out of the pool and back in her room before he was awake.

With one last stroke, she reached out to touch the end wall, intending to turn around, when suddenly a figure appeared in front of her, rising up out of the water. She gave a startled cry, her arms flailing to stop her momentum.

"Good morning." Paul grinned and reached out to steady her. "I see you're an early riser."

She choked and coughed, grabbing for the side of the pool. Their legs tangled, flesh against flesh, his snaring hers. She scooted out of reach. "You scared me half to death."

He slicked his dark hair away from his forehead. "Sorry about that."

Like hell he was. "I didn't think you'd be up yet."

"Most mornings before I leave for the office, I do a few laps just to get the body going. The only exercise I get at work is shuffling papers."

From the look of his physique, he was getting plenty of exercise somewhere. His muscles were long and sleek like those of a swimmer, not bulky like men who worked out in a gym. Matted hair emphasized the planes and angles of his well-sculpted chest.

"Well, I don't want to interrupt your routine."

"You're not. It's nice to have someone to swim with." His gaze dipped beneath the water, making her believe he could see every curve of her body—and every flaw. "Particularly a beautiful woman."

Despite the coolness of the water, her flesh warmed. "I was just getting out anyway. I'll leave the pool to you."

"I'll race you to the other end," he challenged, then eyed her dubiously. "Unless, with your neck injury, you think *vigorous* exercise wouldn't be good for you."

Detecting a subtle reprimand in his voice—or maybe an invitation to a different kind of exercise—she bristled. "I'm sure this kind of *water* exercise is just fine for whiplash. But with or without my injury, you'd be a sure winner. I'm pretty much out of practice. Swimming, that is.'' She was out of practice in other arenas, too. Like flirtation. Attracting a man. Sex.

''Then I'll give you a head start.''

Lord, the man was competitive. That's probably why he had a take-no-prisoners attitude when it came to his law practice.

Not wanting to haul herself out of the pool at the deep end, Melinda had no choice but to rely on surprise to give her whatever edge she could manage. She shoved off from the side and swam as hard as she could for the shallow end, where she'd be able to exit the pool with some grace.

Even at the halfway point she couldn't sense him nearby. Couldn't hear or feel the splash of water as he caught up with her. Was he giving her that big of a lead? She almost felt insulted that he thought she'd be so slow he could give her a head start of half the length of the pool. She'd show him—

He popped up at the steps, shaking the water from his head, waiting for her.

''How did you get here so fast?'' She knew he hadn't been ahead of her. She would have seen—

''Under the water. The pool isn't big enough for a really good workout, so I mostly swim under water. It's good for my lungs. I was with you the whole way.'' His lips canted into one of his patented smiles. ''Nice view.''

She wanted to snarl at him. She really did. But it wouldn't do her any good. So, with as much dignity as she could manage, she walked up the stairs and out of the pool. Let him look his fill. Given all the beautiful women at his beck and call, maybe he'd tire of having her around the house and let her go home before her two weeks were up.

She could only hope so, she thought as she grabbed her neck brace from a glass-topped table and went inside.

LESS THAN AN HOUR after his pleasant, but all too brief, encounter with Melinda in the pool, Paul stepped out of the elevator on the sixth floor of the downtown Reno office building. Across from him were the heavy, double glass doors of DeMarco and Associates, Attorneys-at-Law.

For a man who'd grown up either sweltering in the summer heat or freezing in the winter cold in a bungalow on the outskirts of Reno, he'd done damn good for himself, and Paul was proud of his successful law practice. And his reputation for being a winner in difficult divorce cases.

But keeping pace with his caseload meant he hadn't been able to hang around the house with Melinda and her kids this morning, no matter how much he might have wanted to.

He didn't intend to linger long at the office, though. He'd touch base with his associates, check his schedule with his secretary, be sure everything was under control.

Then he'd get back home to Melinda.

He smiled at the thought as he walked across the

lushly carpeted lobby, greeting Stacy Goodfellow, the attractive receptionist he'd hired a couple of years ago. Stacy was a single mother who'd been in a welfare-to-work program, and was as reliable and hardworking as they came. Paul had never regretted his decision to give her a chance.

"You're looking very chipper this morning, Mr. DeMarco," she said, flashing one of her super-friendly smiles.

"Thank you, Stacy," he replied, without breaking stride. "I'm feeling chipper. How's your little boy?"

"Learning to swim at day camp this summer."

"Terrific."

He headed down the hallway to his corner office with its view of both downtown and the mountains to the west. His secretary was already hard at work.

Ever efficient, white-haired Myrna Wilkinson handed him a stack of message slips, most of them left over from the previous afternoon. He thumbed through them quickly.

"Your sisters called this morning," she said.

He glanced up. "Both of them?"

"Angela says the plumber wants to redo the whole house in copper pipes. It'll cost about four thousand dollars."

Paul winced at the price but knew it had to be done. Angela had been fighting leaks and low pressure for years, and she and her husband were in a tough spot financially with a new baby on the way. "Tell her to go ahead, and send the bill to me."

"And Olivia wants to know who the woman is who has moved in with you."

Hell! Olivia had a grapevine in Reno that rivaled the CIA's. It was probably even more effective, since she wasn't dealing with the fringe element but ladies who regularly visited the beauty salon where she was a part-time manicurist. Paul knew who the source of the information was in this case. The wife of his gardener, who had been working at the house when he brought Melinda home, happened to be the shampoo girl at Olivia's shop. Paul might as well have draped a banner from the top of Harrah's Hotel to announce the news of his houseguest.

He hadn't planned to tell his sisters about Melinda. Not yet. Among other things, at this point there wasn't much to tell. Moreover, a little privacy would be nice. Not that his sisters had ever granted him that luxury. Certainly not when they'd wanted the bathroom and he'd just happened to be using it himself.

Myrna waited expectantly for his answer.

He wadded up Olivia's message. "No comment. Next?"

With a frustrated sigh, Myrna said, "Judge Grayson has switched the McGreggor hearing to this afternoon."

Paul pulled out his pocket computer to make a note of the time and place. He'd get one of his associates to handle the hearing.

"And Mrs. Short screamed at me for ten minutes

on the phone yesterday afternoon, saying she needed more child support from her ex.''

Her ex being Paul's client. ''I'll ask her attorney to talk to her. You shouldn't have to put up with a hysterical woman.''

''She seemed more frightened than hysterical, if you don't mind my saying so.''

''I'll still talk to her attorney.'' Paul represented his clients to the best of his abilities, but he also made a special effort to protect his employees. He didn't like them being badgered. ''What else?''

''Tyler's in the hospital with a bad asthma attack. I put his urgent files on your desk. He's due for an appearance this afternoon in Judge Barker's court. He tried to get the time changed by calling from the emergency room, but says the judge would have none of it. Too many delays already.''

Great. Just what Paul needed. With one associate out sick, instead of delegating his workload, Paul now had to be in two different courtrooms at once. Neat trick if he could split himself right down the middle.

The stack of messages in hand, he went into his office and shrugged out of his suit jacket, hanging it in the small closet near the hidden wet bar, which was well stocked to meet his clients' diverse tastes.

He glanced at his watch. Given the extra cases that had landed on his desk, he'd be lucky to make it home by dinner. If then.

Entertaining Melinda and her children would have to wait. He could only hope she wouldn't take it into her pretty little head to leave on her own. He'd simply have to count on her stubbornness and determination to get back at him to keep her at his house for the next two weeks.

And her promise, of course. He didn't think she was a woman who often broke her word.

Although, he might sleep better at night if she wasn't only paces away in the next room, haunting his dreams.

THERE WAS SOMETHING mildly decadent about lying in the shade beside a sparkling turquoise pool in the middle of the day, sipping iced tea and having nothing to do except watch her children play. Melinda couldn't quite put her finger on what made that feel so wicked.

She was too darn relaxed. Ironically, being trapped by her own lie into living at Paul's house ought to make her tense. It did while he was around. But it was an unpleasant detail she could ignore when he was at work.

At the front of the house, the doorbell chimed. She didn't even have to worry about who had come to call. Tilly would get it.

A moment later, she looked up to see a strikingly attractive woman about her own age standing in the doorway. She was dressed in shorts and a tank top, and had sleek, dark hair that hung past her shoulders and strong features that looked strangely familiar.

Paul's girlfriend? Melinda thought in alarm. What would she think—

"Hi, I'm Olivia Martinella, Paul's sister. And these are my boys, Michael and Steven." The young woman ushered her sons in front of her. "I brought them by to play in the pool. But if I'm interrupting..."

"No. Not at all." Melinda scrambled to her feet, grabbing the neck brace she'd left on the adjacent glass-top table. "I'm Melinda Dumas." Awkwardly, she snagged the brace around her neck.

"Ah, I take it you're the lady from the car accident yesterday." Olivia's broad smile made the familial resemblance to her brother even more obvious.

The younger of her two boys said, "See, I told you she didn't croak."

Melinda stifled a smile. "I'm still breathing, but thanks for your concern."

"That's okay." The child lifted his shoulders in a shrug so classically old-world European it made him appear to be going on eighty. "We didn't get our ride in a T-6 'cause of the accident, though."

Did he wish she'd croaked instead? she wondered, amused. "What's a T-6?"

"A really, really fast plane that goes so fast...." He made a roaring noise and a swooping gesture with his hand. "Fastest plane ever."

"No, it's not," his older brother corrected, jabbing the child with his elbow. "There's lots faster."

By now, Melinda's own children had climbed out of the pool and were standing there dripping in their swimsuits, eyeing the new arrivals. Nancy was squared off against the boys as though defending her territory.

Hastily, Melinda made introductions.

For a few moments, the children gazed at each other with suspicion. Then Michael and Steven claimed their family rights to the pool. Wiggling out of their shorts—revealing swim trunks beneath—they tossed their shirts and towels aside and plunged into the pool. The games were on.

Melinda gestured toward a second deck chair, encouraging Olivia to sit down. ''Your boys are very good-looking.'' Dark haired and dark eyed, like their mother—and uncle.

''They're going to be the very devil to control when they get old enough to do anything with girls besides think they're aliens.'' Smiling, she seated herself and stretched out on the lounge chair. ''Just like my brother was, I imagine.''

Yes, Melinda could imagine Paul as quite the playboy.

''The boys were really distressed about the accident.''

''I didn't realize I'd cost them a ride in a special airplane.''

''Hmm. Don't worry about it. Paul has a couple of friends who fly in the Reno Air Races. The boys will have another chance.''

Tilly scurried out of the house with a plate of freshly baked cookies, and iced tea for Olivia. To the children, she called, ''There're cookies when you get hungry. And I'll make pizza for lunch.''

All four youngsters in the pool cheered as the housekeeper scampered back into the house.

Olivia sipped her tea. "She spoils the kids rotten, and they love it."

"I suppose she thinks of it as part of her job."

In an effort to keep up with Olivia's boys, Nancy climbed out of the pool and did a minicannonball back in. Meanwhile, Ryan stuck safely near the steps, watching the older children.

"Oh, goodness, no," Olivia said. "Or at least that's not all there is to Tilly's story. Didn't Paul tell you?"

"He said she came with the house."

"Well, that's true enough, but there's more." She glanced toward the sliding glass door as though checking to make sure Tilly wasn't within hearing distance. "A few years before she came to work for the previous owners of this house, her husband was driving his pickup with her only child, a daughter, in the front seat, and her grandchildren in the back of the truck. There was an awful accident—south of town on Highway 395—and all of them were killed. Every living member of Tilly's family."

Melinda almost stopped breathing, unable to imagine the pain a woman would suffer by losing her child at any age. Add to that her husband and grandchildren… "That's terrible."

"The worst was yet to come." Olivia's gaze swept over the pool as she checked the children's whereabouts. "The survivors of the other vehicle sued the bejeebers out of Tilly's estate, such as it was. When all was said and done, she didn't have a dime left to her name.''

''How unfair.''

''The guy who owned this place was her attorney. He felt so guilty he hadn't been able to help her more, he hired her as a housekeeper. Then, when he divorced, he insisted that whoever bought the house had to agree to keep Tilly on forever, or at least until she was ready to move into an old folks' home. Paul was the only prospective buyer who bit on the deal.''

My God, it *was* altruism on Paul's part. Melinda never would have—

''Steven!'' Olivia called to her older boy. ''Don't drown your brother. You may need him to support you in your old age.''

With a couple of strokes, Steven put some distance between him and Michael. ''We're just playing around, Mom.''

''No roughhousing. You know the rules.'' Apparently satisfied that her boys would behave themselves for a few minutes, Olivia turned back to Melinda. ''So tell me, how long have you known Paul?''

She slanted Paul's sister a look. ''If you're asking if I'm having a relationship with your brother, the answer is no.''

''I'm that obvious, huh?''

''Yep,'' she agreed, and they both laughed.

''Darn,'' Olivia finally said, still smiling. ''A sister can always hope, I suppose. He seems to have a serious aversion to matrimony.'' Beneath the friendliness in Olivia's voice was a heavy dose of curiosity.

"I'm sure he has all the women he can manage even without offering marriage," Melinda murmured.

"I won't argue with that. But he seems to attract more than his fair share of gold diggers who have long legs but are short in the brains department."

"Maybe that's the kind of woman he prefers."

"I don't think so, not for the long haul. And you certainly don't look like a gold digger to me." Olivia gave her the once-over. "I'd say he's looking for someone really bright, maybe smart enough to get him to rear-end her just to get an introduction."

Melinda wasn't sure whether she should feel insulted or complimented. Despite her chummy routine, Paul's sister was trying to glean as much information about Melinda as she could. Protecting her brother, no doubt. "Trust me, I didn't plan to meet Paul again in quite that fashion."

Her eyes widened. "You already knew Paul when he rammed you?"

Oh, boy, did she! Though *rammed* wasn't exactly the word she'd use. "He was my ex's divorce attorney."

Olivia's demeanor changed to speculation rather than suspicion. "That's interesting. I don't imagine it's such a good way to start a relationship."

"Based on his superb representation of my husband, I was trailing blood from the courthouse all the way home." Her children, too, although she'd tried not to let them know how badly their father—and his attorney—had betrayed them. "Getting rear-ended by him sort of fits right in with getting run over in court."

Olivia grimaced, then shouted at Michael not to splash Ryan. "Someday he might be bigger than you are, honey."

Stifling a laugh, Melinda picked up her tea. Despite the fact that Olivia was Paul's sister, Melinda liked the young woman. Were things different, they might become friends. But she doubted Olivia would be so forthright if she knew of the gigantic suit Melinda planned to file against her brother.

And it was doubly annoying that what she planned made her feel guilty, as though both the accident and being broke were her fault.

Now here she was, camped out in luxury at Paul's house, socializing with his sister and thinking her promise to hang around for two weeks was the dumbest thing she'd ever done. If only she'd just gone back to the ranch, she could have talked with an attorney. The wheels of justice would be in motion. Her neck wouldn't be raw from wearing the blankety-blank brace. And Olivia wouldn't be so damn curious about her relationship with Paul.

The morning slipped into afternoon, and the kids switched from cookies to pizza and swimming to foosball and shuffleboard, where Ryan could finally strut his stuff. For a six-year-old, he had an amazing touch with the disk.

Idly, Melinda wondered if college athletic scholarships were offered in the sport. Probably not.

By midafternoon, everyone retreated inside to the comfort of air-conditioning, and the children started a game of Monopoly.

At the kitchen table, Olivia was preparing to give herself a manicure when she said, "Looks like your nails could use a little sprucing up. Are you game for it?"

"Oh, no, I don't usually—"

"I'm a professional, you know. Top manicurist in the county. Come on, split cuticles give me the willies. No charge."

"Well..." Melinda's fingernails did look rough, and for good reason. Scrubbing floors at the ranch house, training horses and poking around under the hood of a limo did not make for healthy nails, nor did she have much time available for personal grooming.

"Great." When Melinda hesitated, Olivia pulled a second chair next to hers and efficiently laid out her wares, which she'd brought with her in a small suitcase. Talk about being prepared.

Realizing she'd never win an argument with Olivia any more than she would with Paul, Melinda sat down. And why should she object? If she was going to be pampered at Paul's house, why not go all the way? Maybe later this afternoon she'd try out the Jacuzzi upstairs—alone.

She'd dipped her fingers into a bowl filled with a soapy mixture when the doorbell chimed again. Two dark-eyed youngsters appeared, one of them pre-school age, followed by their hugely pregnant mother.

Melinda's brows shot up. "Another sister, I take it?" *Please, God, not Paul's current paramour.*

Olivia grinned. "Hey, Angela, come meet Melinda of the famous car crash. She claims she and Paul don't have anything going on between them. Not that I blame her." She winked at Melinda. "But maybe if we're real nice, she'll take our ne'er-do-well brother off our hands for us."

Choking, Melinda nearly spilled the soapy liquid all over the table. Not that her family was averse to a certain amount of teasing, but these two women were outrageous. Evidently she'd been reading Olivia wrong. The woman wasn't suspicious; she wanted to play *matchmaker,* for heaven's sake.

That was a scheme Melinda desperately wanted to avoid. Paul was the last man on earth she cared to be matched with.

The newly arrived children—Tony, the same age as Ryan, and Victor, two-and-a-half—made themselves at home around the Monopoly board while Olivia plied her art on Melinda's fingernails.

Soon Nancy lost interest in the game—and the boys—in favor of having her own fingernails decorated by a pro.

It had been ages since Melinda had enjoyed so much girl talk, subjects that ranged from the horror and joy of childbirth to coloring hair and using birth control pills. Or, in Angela's case, becoming pregnant while employing every known means of contraception. These last topics had to be delayed until Nancy had wandered away from the impromptu manicure table and gone to take another dip in the pool with the rest of the children, under Tilly's watchful eye.

By the time Tilly came in and started bustling around the kitchen preparing dinner, Melinda's sides ached from laughter, and her neck itched so fiercely, she desperately wanted to yank off the brace. Darn Paul DeMarco for making her seek revenge on him for his evil deeds.

Darn him even more for having such delightful sisters!

PAUL SLOWED as he eased his Mercedes into the driveway. He recognized the cars parked at the curb in front of his house. His sisters were both like mischievous kittens, ready to pounce on any female who showed up within a two-mile radius of him. And they were masters at quizzing the poor woman until she told all of her secrets.

Melinda shouldn't have to put up with a grilling from Olivia and Angela, who made police homicide detectives look like pussycats.

Picking up his briefcase and the bouquet of flowers he'd impulsively bought from a street vendor, he got out of the car and headed for the house.

Once inside, he was greeted by the sound of high-pitched feminine laughter, easily identifiable as that of his sisters. This was followed by a rich soprano voice that slid under his skin like that of a blues singer, promising lingering kisses, warm flesh and long, hot nights. He reacted with startling force. Images of Melinda upstairs, naked in his bed, exploded in his head.

"Uncle Paul!" Six-year-old Tony launched himself at him, wrapping his arms around his waist. Milliseconds later, his little brother, Victor, latched on to one of Paul's legs, the two boys effectively hobbling him.

"Up, Uncle Paul, up," Victor pleaded.

"Sorry, squirt, I don't have any spare hands."

"I dived clear to the bottom today, Uncle Paul!" Tony announced.

"Good for you, kid."

"Michael said I couldn't, but I did anyways."

"Terrific." Using his one unfettered leg, he dragged both boys with him through the formal entryway and into the family room, where game pieces and bits of Lego littered the floor. The remaining children, quiet for the moment, were engrossed in a program on the big-screen TV.

So much for the peaceful, *private* evening at home he'd planned for himself and Melinda.

"Flowers!" Angela squealed from the kitchen table. "Oh, my God, isn't he the sweetest brother ever! He brought me flowers!"

"Uh, no, not exactly," he mumbled, feeling a quick surge of confusion. He tossed his briefcase on a nearby chair and extricated himself from the boys' death grip. "I sort of had in mind—"

"We've been telling Melinda what a thoughtful brother you are, and now look what you've done." Waltzing up to him as gracefully as her pregnant belly would allow, Angela planted a kiss on his cheek.

At the table, Olivia looked as though she were about to burst out laughing—at his expense.

"Yeah, I can imagine what you've been saying," he muttered.

"Thanks for the plumbing," Angela whispered. "Max and I hated to ask...."

"Don't sweat it. He'll get his business going soon."

With a devilish smile, she snatched the cut flowers from his hand. "Why, you know what? These probably aren't for me at all." Whirling, she waddled back to the table. "I just bet he had you in mind."

Melinda, red-faced, shook her head at the extended bouquet. "No, you keep them."

Great, now his sisters had embarrassed Melinda. In his next life he was going to arrange to have nothing but brothers. Carl would never put him in this fix—although Carl's wife, Bea, might, given a chance. Fortunately, since she worked full-time she wasn't likely to show up to meddle in his love life—such as it was—until the weekend.

"Don't you two have to cook dinner for your husbands or something?" he asked his sisters.

Reaching across the table, Olivia patted Melinda's hand. "I think our big, bad brother is telling us to get lost. How 'bout I come back tomorrow and give you a pedicure?''

''Oh, no, you don't have to do that. The manicure was more than—''

Paul took his sisters by the arm and propelled them toward the front door. ''Come on, kids,'' he called to their children. ''Pick a mom, any mom. It's time for you to go home.''

''Aw, Uncle Paul,'' they chorused. ''The Red Dragon is about to eat—''

''Now, guys. You know the rules.'' He shuddered at the thought of what the Red Dragon would devour this time. He really needed to check the censorship controls on his satellite system.

Olivia shrugged from his grasp. ''The children need to clean up their mess. It won't take a minute.''

''I'll do it later, sis. Out.''

Olivia and Angela halted abruptly.

Raising her brows, Angela asked, ''Is she that important to you?''

''Let's just say I'm exploring the possibilities, okay?'' It was way too soon to know where things might lead with Melinda. A man who made his living in divorce court couldn't be too cautious. Marriage was not a future he cared to contemplate, but there were other options.

''If it matters, we like her,'' Olivia said, grinning smugly. ''Among other things, I don't think you'll find her groveling at your feet anytime soon. You just *may* have met your match, big brother.''

He grimaced. ''Go…home…now.''

Standing on tiptoe, they sandwiched him between them, with kisses on his cheeks.

After that, they managed to round up their little darlings and leave with amazing speed. Paul couldn't hurry them fast enough.

Tugging off his tie and shrugging out of his jacket, he returned to the kitchen to find Melinda gathering iced tea glasses and plates bearing cookie crumbs. The flowers, still wrapped in cellophane, lay on the table.

"I'm sorry about all that. My sisters can be pretty overpowering."

"They're a delight. They remind me of how much fun I used to have with Jenny, my brother's wife, before she died. And my sister, Kerry, when we were young."

"Besides the twins, you have a sister, too?" He didn't remember Orly mentioning that.

"A cousin, really. Her parents died when she was five, so my folks adopted her. She's two years younger than I am."

"I've got to say, your family has the most complicated relationships. Babies switched at birth. An adopted cousin. What kind of a secret past do you have?"

"At this point it looks like I'm the only biological offspring my parents have, but that doesn't mean the twins and Kerry are any less their children." She picked up the flowers, smelled them and smiled. "These are lovely, though if you meant them for me, you really shouldn't have. Do you suppose Tilly has a vase for them?''

''I did mean them for you, and, yes, I'm sure she does.'' He slid his hands into his pockets, amazed that Melinda had taken his sisters in stride. Not every woman did. Some felt competitive. Others couldn't handle their interference. And still others were so eager to impress him, they fell all over themselves trying to make friends.

Maybe Melinda didn't care enough one way or the other to give a damn, he thought grimly. She hadn't been all that impressed with the flowers.

Maybe with all the convoluted relationships in her family, she wasn't looking for another complication.

MELINDA SERVED HERSELF a spoonful of Tilly's homemade chicken-and-cheese tortellini with fresh basil sauce and helped Ryan do the same. If she wasn't careful, she'd weigh a ton by the time she moved back to the ranch.

She glanced at Paul, who was sitting at the head of the table, his shirt collar unbuttoned, his sleeves rolled up. ''It was nice of you to ask Olivia and Angela to drop by with their children. Nancy and Ryan enjoyed having other children to play with.''

''I didn't ask them. I hadn't told them you were, uh, visiting.''

''Then how did they know?'' Olivia had been aware Paul had a houseguest. That was curious. And suspicious.

He took the bowl of pasta from Ryan. ''Reno's

basically a small town, and as near as I can tell, Olivia is the town crier, particularly when it comes to keeping tabs on my social life.''

His romantic entanglements, he meant. Melinda didn't like the idea of being talked about in those terms.

''Should I be on the lookout for any more siblings showing up to check me out?'' she asked.

''I've got a brother, but his wife is an assistant hotel manager, so they probably won't drop by till the weekend. Bea has a daughter about Nancy's age.''

''That would have been nice.'' Melinda glanced at her children. ''This is Orly's weekend for the kids, so they might not be here. I know Nancy would enjoy having a little girl her own age to play with.''

Nancy shrugged as though she didn't care. ''Sometimes Dad doesn't come. We might be here, anyway.''

''I'll call him to make sure he knows where you are.'' Taking her daughter's hand, Melinda squeezed reassuringly. ''I know he gets busy and sometimes can't get away. But he always tries, because he loves you.''

The lie stuck in Melinda's throat along with a bite of pasta. She could count on one hand the number of times Orly had taken advantage of the visitation rights his shark attorney had demanded. Why Melinda had bothered to fight the arrangement during the court hearing was beyond her. She should have known Orly was all bluster about wanting to maintain a close relationship with his children. But his actions made her sick to her stomach for her children.

The fact was, if Orly exercised his visitation rights, she'd hate it. Particularly the six weeks each summer when he would take them away from her.

''It can be a pretty big mob scene when all the family converges here at the same time,'' Paul commented. ''I'm glad you and the kids survived the condensed version.''

''Your sisters obviously dote on you.''

''Or maybe it's just that their kids like to hang out around my pool.''

She laughed because she knew that wasn't true. ''How 'bout your parents? Are they still alive?''

''Mom is. She lives in a condo complex that overlooks the river, and insists on keeping her job as a secretary at a wholesale grocery distributor.'' He sounded as though he'd prefer his mother to retire rather than keep on working. ''Dad died when I was fifteen, and she worked two jobs for a while.''

''Oh, I'm sorry you lost your father.''

''Did you get to be the man of the house?'' Ryan asked solemnly.

''Yes, I guess I did. I got my first job then, too.''

''I'm too little to work.''

Her heart breaking, Melinda reached out to her son, caressing the back of his head. ''Right now your only job is to have fun and grow up big and strong and smart, just like you're doing.''

''I had fun today in Paul's pool.''

"You sure did—both of you." She included Nancy in her approving smile.

Thoughtfully, Melinda went back to eating her dinner. It didn't sound as though Paul's family had come from wealth. Indeed, his widowed mother had needed to work two jobs to support her four children.

Melinda glanced past the cut flowers—purple irises, daisies and carnations—toward the opposite end of the table, where Paul was half-hidden from view. Why would an otherwise caring and generous man, who knew how hard it was to be a single mother, intentionally let an ex-husband put another woman in the same desperate financial fix his own mother had experienced?

It made no sense at all.

THEIR AFTER-DINNER reading session didn't last long.

Almost as soon as he'd picked up the mystery and started to read, Paul noted Melinda's eyelids growing heavy, then fluttering closed, despite her best efforts to stay awake.

"I'm sorry," she said, yawning and sitting up on the upholstered lounge chair. "I've been so relaxed all day, and with all that sunshine and fresh air, I just can't keep my eyes open any longer."

She looked so ready for sleep, her eyes slightly puffy and dreamy, that he was tempted to carry her upstairs, lay her on the bed…and join her there. But he doubted she'd approve of his plan.

"It's all right. You're supposed to be getting lots

of R and R while you're here.'' Standing, he offered her his hand to help her up. ''We'll pick up the story again tomorrow night.''

The contact was all too brief before she stood and slipped her hand free.

''Good night, Paul. I'll see you tomorrow.''

He watched her walk up the stairs with natural grace, a feminine sway to her hips. She'd look as good in a long gown as she did in shorts, and would look even better with nothing on at all.

Turning away from the enticing view, he proceeded to close up the house for the night, checking the doors and turning off the lights. He'd had a long day, too, and if Tyler, his young associate, remained in the hospital much longer, the next few days wouldn't get any easier.

The price he paid for success, Paul supposed.

When he got upstairs, he noticed Melinda's light was still on. He felt the urge to knock on her door, ask if she was all right, but he didn't want to risk getting thrown out on his ear. He'd promised he wouldn't enter her room uninvited, lock or no lock on the door.

Shedding his pants, he hung them up in the closet, then removed his shirt, which he carried to the hamper in the bathroom. Tilly took his shirts to the cleaners when—

A cry of pain came from the adjoining room.

Paul didn't hesitate; he burst in on Melinda.

She was standing at the side of the room with one arm raised above her head, her brown eyes wide with surprise. The only clothing on her was a short, red-silk nightie that clung to her curves, leaving little to his imagination. And sending a clear message to his libido.

Unable to speak, Paul simply gaped at her.

CHAPTER FIVE

MELINDA SCREAMED. ''What are you doing in my room?''

''You screamed. I thought—''

''I didn't scream. Well, I did, but not before...'' Using her right hand, she eased her left arm down to her side. The damn thing hurt like blue blazes. ''I was doing my exercises.''

His brows slowly lifted and his gaze swept over her appreciatively. ''Exercises?''

''I'm supposed to walk my fingers up a wall three times a day to get back my flexibility.''

''For your arm.''

''My shoulder, actually.'' Why was she standing here in her too-skimpy nightie, having a conversation with a man wearing even less than... Oh, my, his briefs were soft cotton, intimately revealing what lay beneath.

''Would it help if I massaged your arm?'' He stepped closer.

Her gaze snapped up to meet his. ''No.'' Her voice cracked. ''That won't be necessary.''

''I've been told I have good hands.''

She imagined he did. His chest was top-notch, too,

with dark hair swirling between his dusky-brown nipples and arrowing beneath the waistband of his shorts, where his—

Whirling, she snatched up her light robe. But before she had it all the way on, he was beside her, helping her. The silk fabric slid up her arms and over her shoulders in a whispered caress. He kneaded her biceps and gently rotated her shoulder, his breath blowing warm and sweet on her cheek.

Closing her eyes, she desperately tried not to moan out loud. She didn't want him to know just how good his touch felt, how talented his hands were.

"You shouldn't be here," she whispered. "The children—"

"Are sound asleep."

"But they could—"

"Do they often wake in the night?"

"No, but..." She moaned and rotated her head in a circle to ease the tension she'd felt all day. "You don't have any clothes on."

"They've seen me in my swim trunks. My briefs aren't much different."

Of course they were, though she couldn't seem to find the hole in his logic. That's what lawyers did—confuse people, the same way shifting shadows across the desert deceived, creating mirages. Offering false hope. Lawyers made people think whatever they said was the truth, even when it was a lie.

Smarmy divorce lawyers, in particular.

She stiffened. "I'd like you to leave now."

"Am I hurting you?"

He had hurt her *and* her children. She wasn't going to let him do it again. She intended to get even.

"I'm quite all right now. No need to rescue me." She stepped away from him. "Please close the door on your way out."

He studied her a moment, his gaze intense, fully focused on her, then he ran the back of his fingers lightly down her cheek. "Sleep tight."

Only when he'd left the room, the door clicking in the silence behind him, did she realize she hadn't had her neck brace on. And that there were tears in her eyes—of anger, frustration or need, she couldn't be sure which.

Probably all three.

FRIDAY WAS the first night all week that Paul got home from the office at a decent hour. He was looking forward to a nice, quiet dinner with Melinda, who had been going out of her way to keep her distance from him since the incident in her bedroom a couple of nights ago.

The tactile memory of his hands slipping over the silk that covered her shoulders kept filling his head, along with the knowledge that her flesh would feel even smoother. Warmer. And more tempting.

He opened the front door of the house and collided with Melinda, who was on her way out.

"Whoa," he said, catching her by the shoulders, surprised to see her wearing her chauffeur's uniform. "Where are you going?"

"My friend Natalie, who drives a limo for me, is picking me up. We've got a job for a sweet-sixteen party, and she can't take it. Her son's running a temperature and her husband won't be home till late. Tilly said she'd watch my two while I'm out. I hope that's all right with you."

"You're going to drive?"

"That's what I do for a living."

"But your neck," he sputtered. "If you have another accident—"

"I won't." She tried to edge past him. "I've been driving limos for nearly three years, and you're the first guy who's slammed into me."

"Well, it wasn't a slam, exactly." Not even close. And her neck was fine, he knew. But he still didn't want her to go. Damn it! He wanted her home with him. "How late are you going to be out?"

She looked at him blankly. "I don't really know. I stay out till my client says he's ready to go home. Sometimes these things last past dawn."

"All night?" He didn't like the idea of Melinda staying out all night, even if it was in the line of duty. The city could be dangerous. There were drunk drivers everywhere. She could get mugged. "Your arm hasn't entirely healed yet. Haven't you got someone else who could—"

"Natalie already checked with the college kid I use as a spare driver, but he's not available. So it's me or I lose the job, and the sixteen-year-old's dad is a regular client of mine. Plus, if I don't go, the kids probably can't have their party, because they wouldn't be able to book another limo service at this late date. Which would mean daddy dearest wouldn't be calling Advanced Limo anytime soon, and I'd lose a really good client.''

Normally Paul thought of himself as fast on his feet, always ready with a quick comeback—the result of having a lot of courtroom experience. But at the moment he couldn't think of any way to talk Melinda out of going to work. Except one. An alternative that wasn't all that swift, either.

''I'll drive for you.''

''You'll what?'' she gasped.

''I'll handle the job for you. You're not ready to get behind the wheel again.'' Forcefully, he ushered her back into the house. ''Just tell me where to pick up the kids, and I'll take care of whatever else comes along.''

She shook her head. ''You don't have a chauffeur's license.''

''Actually, I do. I drove a school bus for a couple of years when I was in college. It worked out so I could go to my classes in between taking the kids to school and bringing them home.''

''It's not all that easy to drive a limo. It's long. You have to make wide turns.''

''The bus was pretty big, too.''

''You've never driven Larry.''

''Larry?'' What kind of a client was she talking about? Some guy who liked to maul her? If that was the case, he'd make damn sure—

''I name my limos. Wallowing Wally is in the

shop, thanks to you dinging it. Natalie's limo is Limping Larry. His carburetor sticks. You have to get out and—''

''I think I can handle it.'' With less risk to himself than if he had to teach some Casanova a few things. ''Any other problems?''

He'd worn her down. He could tell by the way her forehead puckered that she was having trouble coming up with any new objections. She looked like an attorney who was about to close her case without having made her argument.

''You don't have a uniform,'' she finally said.

''My dark suit will do. I don't need a hat.''

''Yes, you do. Advanced Limo drivers always wear a cap. Company policy.'' She removed the one from her head and plopped it on his. It perched on top, a good two sizes too small.

A horn honked outside.

''That must be your friend. Wish me luck.''

''Straighten your tie. Grooming's important. And don't forget to—''

He kissed her on the lips, catching the sweet flavor of her shiny lip gloss, the peppermint scent of her shampoo, and winked at her. ''Don't wait up for me. You need your rest.''

OF COURSE SHE WAITED UP for him.

Her arch enemy was driving around in *her* limo with *her* client's daughter on board. The fact that his kiss meant she wouldn't be able to go to sleep anyway had nothing to do with her curling up in a chair in the family room, trying to read a book she'd selected at random, and being utterly unable to concentrate.

Who would have thought such a quick kiss, little more than the brush of his lips on hers, would start her knees knocking and send her heart into palpitations? It wasn't fair.

Extended celibacy must scramble a woman's brains as well as her hormones.

Her head had finally dropped to her chest when she heard a car pull up out front. Glancing at the clock on the mantel, she knew it was too early for Paul to be returning. Not yet one o'clock.

The front door opened.

Grabbing her neck brace, she fastened it in place and hurried to meet him.

"I didn't expect you back—" She came to an abrupt halt. His suit jacket was rumpled, his white shirt dirt-stained, his tie missing, and the shadow of a bruise darkened his jaw. He held her chauffeur's cap wadded up in his hand.

"My God, what happened?" She had visions of the limo wrapped around a lamppost, the occupants bloodied—

"No one mentioned that a limo driver deserves hazardous-duty pay." Paul lurched past her, sinking heavily into the nearest chair. The light from the reading lamp didn't quite reach him, leaving him in shadows.

"Was anyone else hurt?" Pray God her insurance was enough to cover the damages.

"Except for some adolescent noses out of joint, not so you'd notice."

"What are you talking about?"

Leaning back, he gazed up at the ceiling. "Things were going pretty good—until I picked the kids up."

Melinda sat down, too. She didn't think this story was going to have a happy ending.

"I'd barely gotten them into the car when this one kid, an obnoxious sort, asked me—none too politely—to stop off at the nearest liquor store."

"He wasn't planning to buy soft drinks, I gather."

"Not likely. So I told him no. They were all underage."

"Good for you. I would have done the same thing."

"Well, it did set the tone for the evening, I'll say that. The little punk got nastier and nastier." Idly, Paul ran his hand across his bruised jaw.

"He hit you?"

"No, not him. That happened after I took them to the second club." He glanced at her. "I didn't know there were clubs for teenagers in Reno."

"Yep, a couple of them. They come and go."

"Well, I think my little punk got hold of some booze, after all, which made him even meaner. He got into a fight with some kid who was twice his size. Bad decision."

"Oh, my—"

"He wasn't hurt. Much. I managed to rescue him and his friends."

"Thank goodness."

"That's when the big kid clipped me on the jaw."

"Oh, Paul, I'm so sorry."

"It's okay. The boy didn't mean to hit me. He was after the punk. I just got in the line of fire."

"You're being generous about—"

"Of course, by then the cops had showed up. That's when I got the ticket for double-parking."

She swallowed a bark of laughter. "You didn't!"

"Yeah, I did. First ticket I've had in years. I tried to argue my way out of it, but shut up when the cop threatened to arrest me."

"Oh, dear, I am sorry." She giggled. She couldn't help it. He looked so miserable that a warm wash of sympathy rushed through her. "Really, I am."

He eyed her suspiciously. "Come here."

"What?"

Holding out his hand, he repeated, "Come here. I deserve a reward for my valor under fire."

She shouldn't agree to his terms. She really shouldn't. But she found herself slipping her hand in his and allowing herself to be pulled onto his lap.

He skimmed his hand across her cheek, smoothing her hair away from her face. "I took the kids home after the fracas, but they weren't happy campers. I may have lost your client for you."

"It's better that no one was seriously injured. Their father will understand." She hoped. Palming his bruised jaw, she said, "Maybe we should put some ice on that."

"The cure I have in mind will work better."

Slipping his hand to the back of her head, he

brought her closer. Their lips brushed. He adjusted the angle for a perfect fit. She could have objected. Could have pushed away. But the warmth, the sweet pleasure of his mouth on hers sent licks of desire flickering through her to pool low in her body.

Suddenly boneless, she felt her resistance vanish as his skilled tongue slid between her lips, and she leaned into him, moving her hand to his nape. His hair was thick and full, the strands tangling around her fingers. Capturing her.

Greedily, she tasted him. The freshness of mint mixed with the musky scent of his masculinity, a potent combination.

Some small voice of reason buried deeply within her conscience questioned how she could hunger for his taste and still want revenge. Want to take him to court. Make him pay for all of the humilations she'd suffered this past year.

She broke the kiss and braced her hands against his chest. His heart pounded beneath her palm, an echo of her own wildly beating pulse. His eyes had turned to the deepest black of midnight, and his arousal pressed firmly against her thigh.

''I'm sorry you got hurt breaking up a fight while driving my limo.''

His lips tilted in a grin. ''The reward was worth it.''

''Yes, well...'' She scrambled off his lap and stood. ''I don't usually think of myself as a fringe benefit for my employees.''

''I didn't mean that in an insulting way.''

"I know. It's just...it's late." She backed away. How could she have even considered for one single moment... "Nancy and Ryan are early risers."

"I suppose they'll want to be up and ready to go when Orly comes for them."

"Yes, of course." She'd left a message on Orly's phone. He hadn't called back. He rarely did.

"We'll have the weekend to ourselves."

Oh, God, she'd better pray Orly *didn't* pick this weekend to be a loving daddy.

"Good night," she said, fleeing up the stairs.

Smiling, Paul switched off the light and followed her. The evening had ended better than he'd hoped, considering his near disastrous venture into the limousine business.

Melinda might still be wary of him, but a woman that passionate, that responsive to him would be worth the time and energy it took to wear down her defenses. He'd sensed that when they had sat on opposite sides of the negotiating table during her divorce. And again when he'd rear-ended her. Nothing in the past few days had made him change his mind.

Unfortunately, the confirmation of his belief was going to cost him far too many cold showers in the days—and nights—ahead.

He stood in his bedroom, listening to the sounds on the other side of the door. *Two weeks.* Not a lot of time in a man's life. If he'd been smart, he would have garnered a longer promise from her.

Still, he wondered how long it would take her to

realize he knew she hadn't been injured in the accident. And what she would do when she found out.

''NANCY, shouldn't you be getting your things ready to go to your father's?'' Melinda called from upstairs.

Her daughter was sitting cross-legged in the middle of the family-room floor, her concentration intense as she threaded beads for a necklace. ''I'll do it when he gets here, Mom.''

''Where's Ryan?''

''Outside playing shuffleboard by himself.''

''Well, tell him he needs to pack his overnight bag.''

Nancy didn't respond.

Taking a nearby dining room chair, Paul turned it around, straddling it while he watched Nancy at work. ''You don't seem very excited about your dad coming.'' As for himself, he was eager for Orly to arrive. Not that he didn't enjoy Nancy and Ryan's company, but he was looking forward to a weekend alone with Melinda. Maybe he could take her out to dinner, see one of the hotel shows. *Make love.*

Now there was a prospect that would put Orly right at the top of Paul's good-buddy list when he showed up.

''He probably won't come.''

''Your mom seems to think he will.''

Nancy held up the string of beads to examine the progress she'd made so far. ''She always says that.''

Ryan opened the sliding door from the pool deck. ''Anybody want to play shuffleboard with me?''

''Your mom wants you to get ready for your dad,'' Paul said.

''Yeah. I will. Want to play with me?''

Something was definitely out of sync here. Kids ought to be excited about seeing their dad, even if they did see him every other week—the visitation rights Paul had negotiated for Orly. ''Come on in and let's talk a minute, okay?''

Shuffleboard stick in hand, Ryan came inside. ''I just shot five tens in a row.''

''And you figure you're ready to beat the socks off me, huh?''

The youngster grinned at him. ''I'm pretty good.''

Paul chuckled. ''Yes, I guess you are.'' He hooked his arm around the boy and tugged him close. ''You don't really expect your dad to come, do you?''

''Nah. He never does.''

The youngster didn't even sound disappointed, which troubled Paul. ''When was the last time you saw him?''

The child lifted his shoulders in an uneasy shrug. ''I dunno. He sent us chocolate bunnies for Easter.''

Easter? My God, that was three months ago.

''No, he didn't,'' Nancy corrected. ''That was Mom's handwriting on the package. She bought them for us and signed Dad's name.''

''I ate mine. It was good. It had marshmallow stuff on the inside.''

''I like that kind, too,'' Paul said, cupping the

back of the boy's head. "So why do you two think your mom would give you a present and sign your dad's name to it?"

"'Cause she doesn't want us to think he's a dead-beat dad," Nancy said matter-of-factly.

Paul felt the press of dread filling his chest. "Is that what you think he is?"

"Sure," Nancy said, looking up, the wisdom in her brown eyes making her seem far older than her eight years. "But it's okay. Lots of dads sort of forget about their kids after a divorce. But Mom works so hard to make us think Dad cares about us that we don't want to spoil it for her."

The steam went out of Paul's sense of accomplishment that he'd fought for—and *won*—the visitation rights Orly had demanded. Why the hell had the man been so insistent if he hadn't planned to spend time with his children?

To make Melinda squirm, Paul realized.

Some of his clients were like that. Trying, one way or another, to get back at their wives. Paul didn't have to approve. He had to represent them, that's all. And he'd done a damn good job for Orly. Hell, he'd believed Orly meant it when he'd said he wanted to be a good father to his kids.

And Paul had been dead wrong.

Another marriage gone so sour the spouses had become arch enemies. Chalk up another reason why he planned to never put himself in that position.

"How 'bout I take you on at shuffleboard after a

while, champ? I'd like to talk to your mom about something first, okay?''

''I guess. Maybe I can get Tilly to play me. I can beat her easy.''

Paul laughed, admiring the boy's self-confidence. Tilly could play tough, but she was also a doting grandmotherly type who'd blow a game just to see a child's eyes light up with the excitement of winning.

He found Melinda upstairs in her room, sitting on her bed with her legs tucked under her, head bent over as she stitched the brim of her chauffeur's cap back together. The domestic picture brought a lump to Paul's throat. He remembered his own mother mending his clothes, trying to make them last through one more wearing because she didn't have enough money to buy him new jeans or shirts or shoes. Not until her next paycheck. And maybe not then, if the rent was due. Things would've been easier if his father hadn't died.

''Sorry I ruined your hat,'' he said. ''I'll buy you a new one.''

She glanced up, rosy circles of embarrassment coloring her cheeks. ''This one will be fine. No one will notice.''

He sat down beside her on the bed, and her eyes widened in surprise.

''How come you didn't tell me Orly doesn't use his visitation rights?''

''He does. Sometimes.''

''But not often.''

She looked down at her sewing, concentrating on each individual stitch in much the same way her daughter had when threading her beads. Melinda was evading his questions, not wanting him to see the truth in her eyes.

"The kids know he's not coming," he said. "They know he doesn't give a fig about seeing them."

"That's not true! He loves his children. He gets busy, is all. And don't you tell them otherwise!" She spoke in a harsh whisper that seemed to rasp across Paul's conscience. "He's got so many projects going that he can't always get away. The children understand."

"Yeah, they do. But I don't think they understand why you defend him all the time."

Her chin trembled and tears sheened her eyes. She laid down her work. "Do you have any idea how it must hurt my children to wait all day for their father to come visit? All they want is a little attention from him. And he comes so rarely, they've given up on him. A child shouldn't have to give up on his own father."

"It's like he's dead, only he isn't," Paul suggested.

"Sometimes I think it's worse."

Sitting with his feet flat on the floor, he leaned his elbows on his thighs, clasping his hands between his knees. His first emotion when his father had died had been anger. He'd been so mad at his dad for leaving him—leaving his family—that he could barely see through the red haze. Grief had come later. And finally acceptance, if not total forgiveness. Funny what a kid thinks when he loses a parent. That had been when Paul made his own vow never to have children. He didn't want to risk having his own son or daughter repeat the painful experience.

"I think you underestimate your children, Melinda. They've got your ex pretty well figured out. You can be honest with them. Quit defending him."

"You didn't quit. You stood in front of a judge and made him agree that Orly should have the children—*my* children—two weekends a month during the school year and six weeks in the summer. You know what?"

He shook his head, guilt gnawing in his gut.

"Orly had this big real-estate deal going in New Mexico last summer. He was going to make a mint. Not once during the entire time the children were out of school did he call. Not once! Forget showing up to see them for a weekend now and then."

"You could have the agreement amended so he won't get visitation at all—if it's detrimental to the kids."

"Oh, sure. And just what would you like me to use to pay an attorney with? Unless you know someone who'd be willing to work pro bono."

"Is Orly paying his alimony? If not, you could go to the District Attorney—"

"Oh, he faithfully pays the pittance you got the court to agree to. He wouldn't want anyone to look too closely at that again."

"In that case, the D.A. can't help. I'll check around for another attorney." He couldn't represent Melinda himself. It wouldn't be ethical to switch sides in a divorce proceeding. But at least Orly was paying something.

Paul stood up. "I think I'll have a barbecue. Invite the whole family over. If they can come, you'll get to meet Carl and Bea and his stepdaughter. Nancy would enjoy playing with Annie."

"Please don't go to any extra effort on my account or the children's. They'll be fine."

Maybe so, but Paul wanted to make up for the fact that his former client had screwed up big time as a father. Distracting Melinda's children with a lot of action and friends to play with would keep their minds off Orly's absence.

And in the meantime, he'd make sure to give them plenty of extra attention. He'd had a lot of experience as an uncle. Never as a dad.

But if he was given a chance to pick kids to be his own, Nancy and Ryan would be right up there at the top of the list.

Funny, until now he'd never regretted his decision not to have children.

CHAPTER SIX

THE STEADY PLINK-PLINK of a Ping-Pong ball accompanied the happy screams in the swimming pool, the rhythmic sound accented now and then by a shout when one of the players scored a point. More deck chairs had been brought out of storage and were scattered around the pool, colorful beach towels and half-naked bodies draped over them. The rich scent of steaks and hamburgers cooking on a grill filled the air.

The chaotic scene reminded Melinda of the barbecues her family used to have at the Twin Bar Ranch—without a swimming pool, of course. Her father had cooked steaks from beef cattle they'd raised and butchered themselves. The neighbors brought potato salads and six-layer chocolate cakes, home-baked bread and casseroles. Impromptu horse races and calf-roping contests in the corral entertained the teenagers. For the younger children, hide and seek was the game of choice.

Working in the kitchen with Tilly, Melinda smiled as she chopped tomatoes for the salad. Her extended family might not be as large as Paul's, but they'd known how to have a good time.

"You ought to be out there with Mr. D," Tilly

said. ''He doesn't want you wearing yourself to a nub. I've got everything nearly ready.''

''I'm happy right where I am, thanks. I can keep an eye on the kids through the window, and it's a little less hectic here than outside.'' Fewer questions, too, about her relationship with Paul—questions that were increasingly difficult to answer since their kiss last night.

She never should have let that happen. Or enjoyed it so much. Whatever had she been thinking?

Assuming she'd been thinking at all.

Staying at Paul's house was becoming more and more untenable. She'd lied about the accident. She was going to sue him. And all the while he was being the gracious host—even more than that, if she counted his driving the limo for her.

And his kiss.

Behind her a woman asked, ''Anything I can do to help?''

Startled out of her reverie, Melinda turned and smiled at the slender woman with graying hair and chocolate-brown eyes amazingly like those of Paul and his siblings.

''We've got everything under control, Mrs. D,'' Tilly said, opening the oversize refrigerator and bringing out a huge bowl. ''I did up the potato salad first thing, and Melinda here is helping me with the tossed salad.''

''Then you must be Paul's houseguest.'' Smiling, the woman extended her hand.

Nervously, Melinda set aside her paring knife and

picked up a towel to wipe her hands before grasping the one offered to her. ''Mrs. DeMarco, it's nice to meet you.'' Melinda felt as though she was on display to the entire DeMarco clan. She sincerely wished Paul hadn't invited his mother, however close the family might be. It was too much like being taken home to meet Mom, a prospect that gave Melinda the willies, considering the circumstances.

''I met your children out by the pool. They're charming.''

''Thank you.''

''Paul seems quite taken with them.''

''I think he's trying to spoil them. When we all go home—'' she emphasized the temporary nature of their visit, now less than two weeks ''—they're going to miss all this excitement.''

Those eyes that so closely resembled Paul's studied her. Assessing her as a prospective daughter-in-law? Or an unwelcome interloper? ''Yes, well, perhaps he'll invite you back another time.''

Unlikely, after she filed a personal injury lawsuit against him.

Tilly, working at full speed, hustled outside with bags of potato chips, a divided bowl holding three kinds of dip and a tray of veggies. As far as Melinda could tell, Paul's housekeeper had conjured most of the party ingredients out of thin air. She was a marvel, well worth half the price of the house, whatever the market value.

Making herself at home—as well she might in her son's house—Mrs. DeMarco found another cutting board and knife and began chopping baby carrots for the salad.

"Did you meet my son at the office?" she asked casually.

Melinda grimaced. *Here come the questions.* "Not exactly." The first time she had met Paul was across his conference room table, where he'd proceeded to outmaneuver her attorney on every point. But she didn't think that's what Mrs. DeMarco had in mind.

"He put himself through college and law school, you know. I'm very proud of him for that."

"He seems very ambitious." Enough so that for the sake of his client, he'd effectively steal the food out of her children's mouths.

"Ever since his father died, he's taken on a great deal of responsibility for the family. He was so young to try to carry such a burden." Mrs. DeMarco put a large handful of sliced carrots in the salad bowl and selected a cucumber. "He still helps his brother and sisters when he can."

Guilt pricked Melinda's conscience. How could she sue a man who was such a devoted son and brother? But her children needed help, too, largely because of Paul's success in the courtroom.

"I do worry that his work has jaundiced him against marriage," Paul's mother said. "He'd make such a good husband and father."

Melinda suspected a warning in the woman's words, one that, in her case, wasn't necessary. "Evidently he doesn't see it that way."

"Hey, Mama." Arriving in the kitchen, Paul

hooked his arm around his mother's waist and brushed a kiss across her cheek. ''Olivia and Angela have already quizzed Melinda to death, so you can get all the answers you need from them. And no, you can't whip out my baby pictures to show her what a cute butt I had.''

Flushing, Mrs. DeMarco gave her son an affectionate swat on the part of his anatomy in question. ''Well, you did.''

In spite of her best efforts not to, Melinda's gaze slid to the back of his khaki shorts. He still had a great rear end.

A few minutes later, she found herself helping Paul serve up steaks and burgers to more than twenty of his friends and relatives. He appeared to have impromptu parties down to a science. Soft drinks and beer in an ice chest. Buns, mustard, ketchup, pickles, relish, onions and steak sauce on a portable table. And more than enough laughter to fill the entire neighborhood.

Despite the fact she rarely entertained, Melinda felt right at home working beside him. Nephews and nieces accepted her as the designated mom behind the serving table. And if the adults gave her a curious look now and then, they didn't make it obvious.

Olivia and Angela hugged her as though they were her sisters; their husbands made her feel welcome. Paul's brother, Carl, gave a typical warning, telling her to watch out for Paul. Words not unlike their mother's.

It all felt too easy—too comfortable—because she

was a fraud. She was staying at Paul's house under false pretenses.

"Sorry about my nosey family," Paul said when the traffic slowed at the barbecue.

"You have to admit my being here is a little unusual."

His gaze slipped over her like a warm caress. "I find your presence the best thing that's happened around here for a long time."

A mixture of longing and resistance tangled in her midsection. He shouldn't look at her that way. Not in front of his family. And she shouldn't want him to do more than simply look.

Lord, how long had it been since she'd made love? She wasn't so old that she was willing to spend the rest of her life celibate, assuming someone was interested in asking her to do otherwise. But how could she possibly make love with Paul—if he should ask—and then hit him with a lawsuit?

Damn! How had she gotten herself into this fix?

His fault, she reminded herself, but the argument wasn't as convincing as it used to be.

After the guests had left, she took her children upstairs to bed. Despite gallons of sunblock, their skin glowed with a faint sunburn, and their eyes shone from a day of fun and excitement.

Wearing his summer-weight cartoon pajamas, Ryan snuggled under the covers. "The picnic was great, wasn't it, Mom?"

"You sure seemed to be having a good time." Her son had worn himself out trying to keep up with the older children, and his eyes were red-rimmed from fatigue and a heavy dose of chlorine.

"Then, Mom, can we stay here with Paul forever and ever?"

Her breath snagged in her lungs. "No, honey, we're only visiting Paul. We'll have to go home soon." *Very* soon. It was wrong of her to stay here. To let her children get used to this kind of luxurious living. To have a man around who cared about them.

A man she was going to sue.

"Maybe if you were real nice," Nancy suggested, "Paul would be your boyfriend and then we could stay."

Sitting on the side of her daughter's bed, Melinda smoothed the hair back from the child's face. "That's not how it works, sweetheart."

"It could," Nancy insisted stubbornly. Her lower lip jutted out. "If you wanted."

Melinda wasn't going to argue with her children about Paul. "Good night, munchkins. I love you both." Leaning over, she kissed Nancy's cheek, then did the same to Ryan. "I'll see you in the morning."

Tomorrow she'd take the children home to the horse ranch. If Paul wouldn't drive her there, she'd call a cab. Knowing she was going to sue the man, she couldn't stay here any longer. It wasn't right. It wasn't fair. To Paul or her children.

Or to herself.

TILLY BUSTLED AROUND the kitchen the next morning, sorting out the remnants of the party, while Paul sipped coffee and idly perused the Sunday paper at the kitchen table. Melinda hadn't shown up yet. Nor had she come back downstairs after putting her kids to bed last night.

"My, didn't everyone have a good time yesterday, Mr. D? I do believe they all approve of Melinda, don't you?"

"My family can be a little overwhelming." His strategy might have backfired. Rather than providing a distraction for Melinda's kids, he'd scared their mother off. Usually his tactics with women were right on target. This time he might have missed the bull's-eye.

Using a stepladder, Tilly put the leftover stack of paper plates in the cupboard above the stove. "Mercy, too bad we can't harness all that energy those children have, swimming back and forth like little fish. Why, we could light up the entire town of Reno if we could hook them up to the power grid."

"You worked awfully hard yesterday. Why don't you take the day off?"

"Don't you worry about me. There'll be plenty of time for me to rest when they plant me six feet under. I'm in no hurry for that to happen."

Paul was glad to hear that. Though she could easily talk a man's leg off without half trying, he'd miss Tilly if she weren't around.

The doorbell chimed.

"Well, now, who do you suppose that is this early in the morning? Somebody forgot something yesterday, I imagine.'' Setting aside a box of plastic forks and knives, she headed for the door.

''I'll get it.'' Paul shoved back from the table. ''You go on with what you're doing.''

The man standing on his front porch was a good two or three inches taller than Paul—which made him over six feet—and outweighed him by twenty pounds, all of it muscle. Paul got an uneasy feeling that raised the hair on his nape.

''May I help you?''

''I'm Zachary Dumas. I'm looking for my sister, Melinda.''

Surreptitiously, Paul checked to see if the man was carrying a shotgun behind his back. Seeing none, he opened the door wider and introduced himself. ''Melinda and the kids aren't up yet. There's coffee on if you'd like.''

''No thanks.'' He strolled into the living room, giving the interior of the house a once-over. ''Nice place you have here.''

''Not as much land as you have, of course, but it does me well enough in the city.''

Zach stopped in front of the fireplace, turning back to face Paul. ''You know who I am?''

''As I recall, you're the cattle rancher, and your brother Zane raises the Arabians.''

''She told you about us?''

''Actually, her former husband and I had some extensive discussions about Melinda's brothers and the ranch you all own together. I was Orly's divorce attorney.''

Paul's admission dropped between them like a balloon filled with sand.

Lines of confusion furrowed Zach's brow. ''First of all, Melinda doesn't own any portion of the ranch, not since Orly talked her into having us buy her out so they could invest in that limo service that was going to make them a fortune. Or so Orly claimed. And secondly—''

''Wait, let's stop right there. You're saying Melinda doesn't derive any income from the ranch?''

''Not a dime. Zane and I cashed her out, in spite of a whole helluva lot of qualms. No ranch makes a great profit. In the case of the Twin Bar, we've always plowed whatever we got back into more beef. Or Arabians, in Zane's case.''

''But it's still an asset, right? As far as Melinda is concerned?''

''Nope. Melinda signed over the title. It's recorded, if you want to check.''

Paul sat down heavily on the arm of the nearest chair. How could that be? Orly had been so adamant that Melinda had her own sources of income. That she was lucky *he* wasn't going to sue for support, given his own income was erratic. Or so he'd claimed.

''Let's get back to the more important question,'' Zach said. He hovered over Paul, his fingers stuffed into his jean pockets. ''Given that you were snake-oil Orly's attorney, why in hell has she moved in with you?''

Shaking his head, Paul tried to come to terms with

what he'd just been told. "No, it's not what you think. I hit her—"

"You what?"

Paul held up his hands, palms outward in a gesture of surrender. "I *accidentally* rear-ended her limo last week. Nothing serious," he hastened to add. "But she got a mild whiplash injury." So mild it had all been an act, but Paul wasn't going to tell her brother that. It was his little secret—and Melinda's.

"My fiancée said something about seeing Melinda at the hospital. She's a doctor. But I didn't think—"

"Melinda didn't have anyone to care for her at the ranch. Apparently your brother's out of town."

"Out of the country," Zach grumbled, as though he wasn't pleased with his brother's absence.

"I was sure the doctor didn't want Melinda to be doing any heavy lifting or running after the kids. She needed to rest and recover."

Some of the tension visibly eased from Zach's shoulders. "So you're taking care of her?"

"My housekeeper is doing most of the work." Paul would have loved to do more, like give her a massage now and then, or a foot rub, but Melinda didn't seem all that willing.

"That's good," Zach said with a nod. "She works too hard as it is, what with the limo service, the kids and taking care of Zane's big house even when he's not there. She could use someone looking out for her."

Exhaling a silent sigh of relief, Paul relaxed a little. "I was hoping you'd feel that way." Better than having Zach punch his lights out, which he could probably do, given adequate motivation. And Paul's jaw hadn't entirely recovered from the bruising it took while he was playing limo driver.

"How 'bout you and my sister? Beyond just being a nice guy, is there anything else going on I should know about?"

Paul weighed the relative merits of being honest, and decided that if he and Melinda ever did get together, it would be better to be up front with her brother. "I'd like there to be more, but so far Melinda's not interested." Except for that one kiss, which Paul felt no compunction to reveal.

"The past couple of years have been hard on her. She deserves to have the cards fall in her direction for a change."

"Might be she needs a whole new deal." If Orly had misled him about the ranch and visitation rights, what other misinformation had his client foisted off on him?

Nodding, Zach ran his hand along the back of his neck. "I could use some of that coffee now, if it's not too much trouble. I'd like to wait to see Melinda myself. And the kids, of course."

"Sure." Paul gestured toward the kitchen. "My housekeeper uses a special vanilla-flavored blend that's terrific."

STEPPING OUT OF HER ROOM, Melinda heard voices downstairs. Surely she wouldn't have to run the gauntlet of yet another set of DeMarco relatives. So far this morning she'd sorted most of her clothes and personal items, ready to pack up for home. But her need for coffee was paramount at the moment.

Checking to make sure the prickly neck brace was on properly, she walked toward the voices in the kitchen. The sweet smell of freshly baked bread wafted around her. Tilly was a domestic marvel.

"Zach!" she cried, spotting her brother and flying into his outstretched arms. "What are you doing here?"

"I came looking for you, sis."

She winced. "I guess I should have called you." Under the circumstances she'd been reluctant to have her family get wind of her scheme, certain they wouldn't approve.

"No, you should have let Mom know where you were. She called the ranch and talked to Ramón. Then, in a panic, she called me."

"I'll phone her right away."

"It'd be better if you went to see her. Ramón told her you'd had an accident, and she was really worried."

"I'll go see her. I promise." Melinda took the mug of coffee Tilly handed her, thanking her with a nod. "Actually, your timing is perfect, Zach. I was just starting to pack. Would you mind running the kids and me home? It would save Paul a trip."

At the far end of the table, where he'd been sitting quietly, Paul abruptly stood and took a step toward her. "You're leaving? I was hoping—"

"I appreciate your hospitality. The children have had a wonderful time, but—"

"I don't think that's a good idea, sis."

Her attention whipped back to her brother. "Why on earth not? We've been here a week—"

"Leslie tells me soft-tissue injuries like yours take a long time to heal."

"But I need to be at the ranch," she protested.

"Ramón can do anything that needs doing."

"The house—"

"Nobody's heard from Zane, so he's not coming home anytime soon, which doesn't make Mom happy, either. It's no big deal if a little dust accumulates, is it?"

Frantically, she shifted her gaze back and forth between the two men. *A conspiracy!* Damn it! How could they have become such close buddies this fast? Didn't Zach know Paul was the shark lawyer who'd cost her so much?

But if she started to whine now and admit what she had in mind, the whole lawsuit would fly out the window. There would be no money for her to rent a small house in town where the children could be near their friends. No money for school clothes, come fall. Santa Claus would be a bust again this year.

"I'd really like to go home," she said tightly.

"Oh, I do wish you'd stay longer," Tilly said. "This house is so quiet with only Mr. D in it. And I do love having the little ones around."

Dear heaven, Tilly had unwittingly joined in the conspiracy, leaving Melinda without a single ally.

"Give yourself a little more time to heal," Paul urged. "The children are enjoying themselves. It doesn't sound like there's any particular urgency for you to return to the ranch. Enjoy your chance to relax."

"He's right, sis." Zach pulled out a chair at the table for her. "Think of it as a well-deserved vacation."

"I'd be happy to take you and the children to see your mother, if you'd like," Paul volunteered. Tilly handed him a plate with fresh homemade muffins on it, which he set in front of Melinda, tempting her. "We could do that this morning after the kids have breakfast, then have a late lunch somewhere. Maybe run up to Pyramid Lake for a ride in my boat. A nice, easy ride that wouldn't jar your neck."

"You've got a boat?" Zach asked.

"Yeah. I use it for water-skiing usually, but there's no law that says I have to rev up the engines."

"No fooling. I went water-skiing once a long time ago. Almost broke my neck going over a jump." Settling back into his chair, Zach proceeded to relate the tale from his adolescence.

Melinda rolled her eyes. Somehow the two of them had decided she'd stay at Paul's, despite her objections.

God, men were so damn bossy!

She couldn't figure a graceful way out of the mess she'd created for herself. Not without blowing her plan.

"THEN I JUMPED into the deep end and Paul catched me. Then I beat this big kid at shuffleboard, 'cause he didn't use any..." Puckering his forehead, Ryan paused for a breath as he tried to remember the word his grandma had taught him. "*Finesse.* He just whacked it real hard."

"And you know better than that, don't you?" Eleanor Dumas cuddled her grandson closer to her on the couch where they were sitting together, Nancy tucked under her opposite arm.

The town house she and Melinda's father lived in was neat as a pin, the knickknacks Eleanor had collected over the years displayed on bookshelves and tabletops—including a lopsided clay flower pot Melinda had thrown in her high school ceramics class and painted blue to match the spring wildflowers that grew around the ranch.

Although the town house was much smaller than the ranch house where Eleanor had raised her four children, she seemed to be thriving in the new environment. Plenty of neighbors to visit, card games to play and a championship, senior-circuit shuffleboard league.

As Ryan continued to chatter, Melinda smiled at his animated conversation. Normally he was a quiet child, even with someone he knew. A week at Paul's house had done him wonders.

She glanced over at Paul, who had made himself at home and was browsing through her father's illustrated *History of World War II* encyclopedia. He seemed to fit in anywhere—flipping burgers on a barbecue, lying on the living room floor and putting together Lego models with the same intensity as her six-year-old, or visiting in her parents' home.

And advocating for his clients in a courtroom, she reminded herself.

"What about you, Nancy?" Eleanor asked, turning to her granddaughter. "Have you been having fun at Paul's house, too?"

She held up her fingers, waggling them in the air. "Aunt Olivia painted my nails."

"Oh, my, aren't those fancy. *Aunt* Olivia?" Eleanor shot Melinda a questioning look.

"My sister," Paul explained. "She views it as part of her God-given responsibility to check out any woman who happens to show up at my house. I'm afraid she and my younger sister, Angela, gave Melinda the third degree."

"I see." Eleanor's brown eyes twinkled. Although she was past seventy, her vision hadn't dimmed, or her sense of humor. Only her hair, now laced with gray, and an increased number of wrinkles lining her face, gave away her age. "I remember Hamilton's sister giving me a dreadful time when we first started dating."

"Paul and I aren't dating, Mother," Melinda quickly interjected.

Paul's grin came just as swiftly. "That's true. But maybe I should rectify that situation."

Melinda flushed.

Her mother said, "Oh, I think that would be lovely. Melinda needs to get out more."

"Can I come, too?" Nancy asked.

"No." Popping up from her chair, Melinda went to the window to peer outside. "I can't imagine what's keeping Dad." The sooner he returned from wherever he was, the sooner she could leave.

"Oh, he's probably hanging around with his cronies, watching a checkers game." Eleanor gave both children a squeeze. "I tell you what, little ones. Why don't you show Paul around, take him over to the recreation center, and maybe you'll find Grandpa."

On cue, Paul stood, extending his hand to the children. "Come on, kids. I think your grandma wants to have private words with your mom."

"Oh, dear. Was I that obvious?"

As slick as glass, he leaned down to brush a kiss on Eleanor's cheek. "I'm interested in seeing the complex, anyway. I wanted my mother to move into a place like this, but she opted for a small apartment house. She thought it was wasteful to live on a golf course when she'd never even owned a golf club."

"You're a sweet boy, Paul DeMarco. You come see me anytime, won't you? And don't feel you have to wait for an invitation from Melinda."

"I'll make it a point to drop by when I'm in this part of town." Chuckling, he walked out the door hand-in-hand with the children.

Melinda fumed. This whole scheme of hers wasn't working out according to plan. The way things were going, when she sued Paul, her whole family would testify for the *defense*.

After Paul had left, Eleanor stood and went to the

window, watching him and the children stroll down the curving street lined with well-kept homes.

"Your young man does seem very nice," she said pensively.

"He's not my anything, Mother." Out of guilt, Melinda spoke a little too sharply.

Eleanor turned away from the window. "You know I worry about all my children. I just want you to be happy."

"I know, Mother. I'm sorry I snapped at you." Stress—and a lawyer who had bulldozed his way into her life—did that to a woman.

"I worry about Zane, too. I do wish he'd call to let us know he's all right."

Standing, Melinda wrapped her arms around her mother. "I worry, too. We just have to believe he'll work through his grief and come out of it stronger."

Her mother's shoulders shook slightly, as though she were fighting tears. "He doesn't even know that I'm not his—"

"You *are* his mother, just like you're Zach's and mine. Neither one of the twins will ever be able to think of that singer as their *real* mother. Not in any sense other than biological. They love you."

"I know, dear. It just feels so strange, after all these years, to learn the boys weren't my babies. I loved them right from the first—" Her voice broke.

"It's all right, Mom."

"If only Zane would come home, I know I'd feel better."

Out the window, Melinda spotted the children,

Paul and her father returning. The two men were chatting amiably as though they were lifelong buddies. Was there anyone in the world Paul didn't get along with?

CHAPTER SEVEN

"COME ON, KIDS. Upstairs to bed."

Weary after leisurely hours of boating on Pyramid Lake, Nancy and Ryan followed their mother's instructions without argument.

Paul caught Melinda's arm before she disappeared upstairs with her children.

"When you've got the kids tucked in, I'd like to talk with you."

"It's late. It's been a long—"

"This is important. Please." He had to know how badly Orly had lied to him, and whether, as Orly's attorney, he'd inadvertently cheated Melinda out of what should have been rightfully hers. "I'll wait for you on the deck."

Cocking her head, she studied him for a moment, her soft brown eyes filled with questions. "All right. Give me a few minutes."

While he waited, Paul uncorked a bottle of his favorite chardonnay, then took the wine and two glasses out to the umbrella table by the pool. It was one of those soft summer nights, still warm enough to feel comfortable wearing shorts. The air was filled with the fragrance of desert sage and foothill pines mixing with the scent of cultivated roses from the neighbor's yard. The sounds of the city were muted. Somewhere among the nearby homes, a dog barked and was shushed by its master. Overhead, a three-quarter moon shone down, painting the rocky terrain of Mount Rose with irregular shadows and turning Paul's swimming pool to liquid gold.

He poured himself a glass of wine. It was a night meant to be shared with a woman.

For a week and a day, he'd been trying to convince Melinda he wasn't the ogre she believed him to be. That he didn't deserve the anger that made her want to get even, to threaten by implication a personal-injury suit. He didn't have much time left to prove his case.

And now he'd discovered she might be justified. If her brother's statements were true, Paul had based the financial package that closed out Melinda's divorce on false information.

He didn't relish that possibility.

The sliding door opened behind him, and he turned. She'd brushed her windblown hair back into order, the natural curls gently kissing her cheeks and curving beneath her shell-like ears. Her sandaled feet and bare legs looked suntanned in the moonlight. Smooth. Perfect for a man to caress.

Her eyes were wary.

''What is it you wanted?'' she asked.

You. The intensity of her tone surprised him.

He poured wine for her, then handed her the glass.

"Your brother and I had an interesting conversation before you came downstairs this morning."

"I gathered as much."

"He tells me you don't own any part of the Twin Bar Ranch."

"That's right. Orly insisted I sell my share so we could buy the limo service, one of his many grand schemes that were going to make us a fortune."

"During the divorce, Orly showed me deeds to the Twin Bar with your name on them."

"They must have been old documents."

Evidently, and Paul hadn't taken the time to check for any changes in ownership. He carried such a big caseload and had so many clients that some days the paperwork overwhelmed both him and his staff. Still, he usually paid attention to important details. Details that would shift the balance of assets in a marriage that was about to dissolve.

"But you do own the limousine service," he continued.

"Me and the bank." Taking a sip of wine, she settled into a chair at the table, sitting half in moonlight and half in shade. "We had to take out a business loan in order to buy the service. Then there were business licenses, vehicle licenses, corporate registration. The list was endless. Then Orly discovered both limos had more than a hundred thousand miles on them. The speedometer was going around for the second time."

"So you hadn't gotten a very good deal on the company."

"Not exactly. It also meant we had to buy two new limos, which I'm still paying off. A gallon of blood per month about covers the debts," she quipped, but without a trace of humor.

Paul grimaced. It didn't sound as though Orly were a very good businessman. "But you do manage to make a living with your limos?"

Placing her glass on the table, Melinda turned toward him. "I don't know what Zach told you. I can barely make ends meet. Basically I'm broke. That's why I moved into Zane's place after I sold off the house to pay Orly's gambling debts."

"What gambling debts?" A niggling headache threatened at the base of Paul's skull. It had nothing to do with getting too much sun during the afternoon, or the half glass of wine he'd drunk this evening, and everything to do with a former client's lack of candor.

And his own inattention to details.

"Orly had a surefire system to beat the casinos." She laughed bitterly. "Is that an old story or what? There have to be a thousand different *systems,* and none of them work at the roulette wheel or the blackjack table or anywhere else. But you couldn't tell Orly that."

The situation was worse than Paul had feared. Much worse. And he was responsible.

No wonder Melinda had been willing to fake a neck injury in the hope of getting back at him. *Revenge* was an ugly word. He hated to think that in this case he deserved it. Yet he'd done his ethical duty, representing his client as best he could. He'd won. In the adversarial court system, the opposing attorney had an obligation to present facts that countered his arguments.

Except Melinda's attorney had been incompetent.

He swallowed hard against the knowledge that his success in Melinda's case had been a shallow victory. "Orly didn't mention he gambled."

"He wouldn't. He viewed gambling, like all of his schemes, as a sure thing."

Melinda came to her feet, stunned to realize Paul had been unaware that his actions would throw her into desperate financial straits. She could hear the surprise in his voice, see the concern in his expression. He'd believed Orly's lies.

Just as she had during their fast-paced courtship and early years of marriage.

Damn it! Paul was the hotshot attorney. He *should* have known. If nothing else, he damn well should have checked.

"Tell me, Paul, do you ever represent women in divorce cases? Or do you work exclusively for the old-boys' club?"

"Of course I represent women. But I suppose I've developed a reputation and a special affinity for the problems men face in a divorce proceeding. They can get taken to the cleaners if they're not careful. And I do believe men ought to have visitation rights with their children."

"Well, you certainly did your number on me, didn't you? Orly doesn't send me enough money to even visit the cleaners, and you know what he does with his cherished visitation rights.'' Suddenly the long day and the strain of living a lie weighed her down. ''If there's nothing else you wanted to discuss, I think I'll go up to bed now.''

He toyed with his wineglass, moonlight glancing off the crystal and splintering the light. ''No, I guess that's all I had on my mind.''

Regret slid through her as she went inside. A beautiful moonlit night and Paul's only interest was in her financial situation.

It should have been a romantic moment. A time for a man and woman to share intimate secrets, whispered words. They could have so easily slipped into the cool water of the pool, the privacy of darkness eliminating the need for swimsuits. Or modesty.

With such a mood, there would be no racing from one end of the pool to the other. The only competition would be in the way they stroked each other. Slowly. With tenderness. And the kisses they would share.

But she was here because of a lie.

Melinda paused at the doorway and turned back to where he was standing in the shadows. ''Why is it you've never married?'' she asked, knowing she shouldn't let her curiosity get the better of her.

''More than half of all marriages end in divorce. The relationship turns bitter, the spouses at each other's throat. You know that.''

''You don't think love can overcome that?''

"Every client I've ever had thought he was in love when he got married."

"So you won't take the risk."

"I have responsibilities to my family. And frankly, from what I've seen, love is overrated."

"You love your family. I've never seen anyone who cares more about siblings, nephews and nieces. Your mother. Is that kind of love overrated, too?"

"All right. *Romantic* love is the problem. It can get a man—or a woman—in deep trouble. It can shatter a person's life and his spirit. I see that every day."

She had to concede he was right. Worse, she was at risk of having the same thing happen to her if she allowed her heart free rein. As usual, the resident attorney had won his argument.

With a nod, she left him standing there.

In her room, she blinked away the burn of tears in her eyes. A long time ago she'd dreamed, as adolescents do, of a knight in shining armor in the guise of a cavalry officer, coming over the rise to rescue her. To protect and defend her. Take care of her. To love her beyond all else.

She'd fallen in love and married Orly, then found that dream to be false. She didn't dare make that mistake again.

Especially with a man who believed in divorce, not marriage.

SHOVING OPEN THE DOOR to his office reception area the next morning, Paul marched past Stacy Goodfellow with barely a nod and headed directly for Tyler Cassidy's office. The young man, whose mind was as brilliant as his glasses were thick, was sitting behind his desk.

''Good, you're here,'' Paul said.

''Yes, sir. I'm sorry about being out so much last week. The doctor has changed my—''

''Don't worry about it.'' Paul waved off the young attorney's apology. ''I want you to pull the Orly Haas file. I want everything in there, every statement we made to the court or piece of paper we filed, to be double-checked and checked again for accuracy. We don't take the client's word or our own unless it's confirmed by an original source.''

''There's a problem, sir?''

Damn right there was, and Paul was going to set things straight. ''Make it a top priority, Tyler.''

Tyler closed the file he'd been working on and put it aside. ''Yes, sir.''

Doing an aboutface, Paul went down the hallway, stopping at Myrna Wilkinson's desk. Before she could open her mouth to greet him, he said, ''Get me A.J. I've got a job for her.'' In the divorce business it wasn't unusual to use a private detective to track down philandering spouses and hidden funds. A.J. was one of the best.

By the time Paul had hung his coat in the closet, the intercom buzzed. It was Myrna letting him know Adrian Jordan was on the line.

Within minutes, Paul had the ball rolling. Orly Haas was about to become an open book. If he'd misled Paul or hidden anything from the court, they'd damn well know it soon.

Though not soon enough to have protected Melinda from a perjurious spouse when she needed it.

''Call me back whenever you get something,'' he urged the detective. ''Day or night.''

''You got it, Mr. D.'' A.J.'s voice sounded like an angel, but Paul knew she was more like a tiger when she got her teeth into a job.

By noon, Paul had seen two clients, counseled one of his associates on a complicated divorce settlement she was working on, and returned a half-dozen phone calls from clients and opposing attorneys.

When Myrna buzzed him with yet another phone call, he was hoping this one wouldn't mean trouble. No such luck. The owner of the body shop that was repairing Melinda's limo gave him the bad news.

Hanging up, Paul called home. He swiveled his chair around to look out over the city while he waited for Tilly to summon Melinda to the phone. Streams of vapor rose from the roofs of office buildings, a sign that air conditioners were hard at work.

''Yes?'' Her sweet voice held a note of apprehension.

''I just spoke with the owner of the body shop that's working on your limo.''

''I hope it's ready. They've had my car for a week. Without wheels, I'm beginning to feel like a prisoner, and the lack of income isn't helping my bank account.''

''The bumper is fixed and rechromed.'' Out the

window, he watched a plane circle toward the mountains, probably en route to the South Tahoe airport. ''Unfortunately, he's found another problem.''

''What problem? If it's just another scratch, tell him to—''

''It's serious. The frame is bent.''

There was a long pause on the other end of the line. ''You didn't hit me hard enough to bend the frame, for heaven's sake.''

''I don't think so, either, but I'll still cover the repairs. The body man tells me when they take a regular chassis and extend it for a limo version, manufacturers sometimes cut corners. They don't provide enough bracing, which leaves the vehicle susceptible to breaking in half.''

''Oh, God...'' she groaned. ''Are you sure he's not trying to jack up his price, fix something that isn't actually broken?''

Paul swiveled back to face his desk, noting the growing stack of case files covering the surface. ''I've used this firm before. Rutledge comes highly recommended and has always been entirely honest with me. I plan to drive over there so I can see what he's talking about.''

''I want to go, too.''

''I'll take care of—''

''It's my limo, Paul. My livelihood, such as it is.''

She was right, of course. Melinda had more at risk here than he did.

He glanced at his watch. ''Okay, I'll pick you up in fifteen minutes. I'm scheduled to be in court at two, but we'll have time to take a look, and you can decide what you want him to do. Ask Tilly to baby-sit the kids."

MELINDA WAS WAITING when Paul pulled into the driveway. As she climbed into his Mercedes, a blast of cool air swept over her, raising gooseflesh along her arms.

Dread gnawed at her midsection.

It wasn't possible the little tap Paul had given her limo had resulted in such major damage. She'd barely felt the collision. And now if the limo couldn't be easily repaired, even her marginal income was at stake.

She slanted a glance at Paul. He'd hung his suit jacket on a hook in the back seat and was wearing a long-sleeved white shirt with a conservative silk tie. His hair was neatly styled, trimmed just above the collar line. An expensive watch with a platinum band cuffed his wrist as he drove with ease through residential streets that featured homes worth megabucks.

All in all, he presented a powerful image. No doubt that's what he intended for his afternoon court appearance—to impress the opposition and the judge.

Stifling a sigh, she admitted he impressed her, too. More than a man who didn't believe in marriage should. She wasn't the sort who could simply have a casual affair. Because of her children, that choice was out of the question. Not that Paul had pressed her on that issue—to her surprise. And disappointment, she conceded.

All he'd done was be kind and considerate to her and her children, possibly to avoid a lawsuit. Hardly a great foundation for a relationship.

In return, she'd planned the lawsuit he hoped to avoid.

"You know you couldn't have done major damage to my limo in that accident, don't you?"

"We'll see what the body man says."

"I have a huge deductible." And a minuscule bank account.

"Don't worry about the money. I'll take care of it."

"Why, if it wasn't your fault?"

He was silent as he turned onto old Highway 80. "Maybe it's my fault you have to drive a limo at all."

That momentarily halted both the worries and sensual thoughts cycling nonstop through her head. "What are you saying?"

"That maybe in the case of Haas vs. Haas, I had blinders on while I represented my client."

Hope surged through her. "Are you saying you want to reopen my case?"

"That's not an easy thing to do once a court order has been issued." He wheeled into the parking lot beside Rutledge Body Shop, a one-story building painted in rainbow stripes that had long since faded to pastel. "Let's see what Rutledge has to say."

Great. He'd evaded her question. That probably

meant he wasn't planning to do anything. And why should he? He'd won the case for his client, right? That was his job.

Her limo was parked in front of an open bay door, the chrome bumper gleaming—just the way it had before the accident, if her recollection was clear. And right after it, too. As they both examined the limo, their distorted reflection in the chrome compressed their heads to the size of grapes and elongated their torsos. A perfectly matched couple, she thought with grim amusement.

''What about this frame problem he told you about?'' She started to kneel to look under the body, but Paul caught her arm, his hand firm at her elbow.

''Let him put it up on a hoist. It'll be easier to see.''

Easier on her knees, too, she realized. Instead of shorts, she should have worn jeans to hang around a body shop, but she'd only taken time to brush her hair and freshen her makeup after Paul's call. And put on her neck brace, of course. She was really getting tired of being held prisoner by the damn thing.

''Howdy, Mr. DeMarco.'' The body-shop owner sauntered over to them, his blue overalls stained with grease, his navy knit cap pulled down to cover the tops of his ears.

''This is Ms. Dumas,'' Paul said by way of introduction. ''The owner of the limo. She'd like to take a look at the damage.''

''Sure thing.'' Moving with the speed of a desert tortoise, Rutledge slipped behind the wheel, started the engine, then jockeyed the limo around to drive it inside. Once there, he got out, and a few moments later, with a swish of compressed air, the vehicle rose up on the hoist.

Paul and Melinda peered underneath, not that Melinda knew what she was looking at.

''This here's the spot with the problem.'' Rutledge tapped a pencil to a metal bar that ran the length of the limo. ''Afore we send out a finished job, we always take an overall look, see that we didn't miss nothing. That's how we found them two pieces out of alignment.''

''It doesn't look too bad to me,'' Melinda said with more than a little wishful thinking.

''Looks can fool you. You was to take another rap on the rear end like you did, or even go over a bump in the road, that's a weak spot. It could give way anytime, maybe break in two or telescope the back end right into the front seat.''

''Did the accident I had with her last week cause the damage?'' Paul asked.

The mechanic scratched beneath his knit cap. ''Hard to tell. Could be. Then again, could've happened before that.''

''Thanks for the definitive answer,'' Melinda grumbled. ''Is it fixable?''

''Yep. I can put you a brace right here. Another one here.'' Again, with his pencil, he showed her. ''You need one on the other side, too.''

''It's broken, as well?'' she asked.

''Not so's I can see without an X ray or such. But

if it was me, I wouldn't trust it none. Whoever built this rig shouldn't have, neither.''

Melinda couldn't remember the manufacturer's name offhand, nor could she bring herself to ask how much the repairs would cost.

''Go ahead with the job and put it on my tab,'' Paul said.

''It'll take a little welding, is all,'' Rutledge said.

''It doesn't seem fair that you have to pay the cost,'' she protested to Paul.

''Don't worry about it.'' He slid his arm around her shoulders, hugging her in a reassuring gesture. ''We'd better get going. Judges don't like to be kept waiting.''

It'd be so easy for her to lean on him all the time, enjoy the feel of his strength wrapped around her. Let him make the decisions, pay the bills. But for better or worse, it was *her* limo service. *Her* responsibility.

''We bought another limo at the same time we bought this one, Mr. Rutledge.'' Orly's brainstorm, for which she'd be paying the rest of her life. ''If I had that brought over here, would you check it out for me?''

''Be happy to.''

She took a step away from Paul. ''I'm going to call Natalie, get her to bring Limping Larry over here.''

''You may be asking for trouble if Rutledge finds the same problem.''

''I'd rather be safe than sorry. I don't want my

friend driving an extended limo that could collapse into a two-door coupe with a little whap on the rear end.''

He checked his watch. ''I really need to get to the courthouse.''

''You go ahead. Natalie will give me a lift home after Mr. Rutledge checks out Larry.''

''Ma'am, I don't usually work on folks, you understand, just cars.''

She smiled at the body-shop owner. ''It's okay. Except for his carburetor, Larry's very well behaved.''

RUTLEDGE'S INSPECTION didn't take long, and for reasons Melinda wasn't going to question, he gave the limo a clean bill of health—except for the carburetor, which died twice while he was driving Larry onto the hoist.

''You might want to take him to a mechanic, have that looked at,'' he suggested.

''I have. Several times.'' She shrugged helplessly. ''When I take him into the shop, he runs beautifully, and then breaks down on the way home.''

Natalie patted the hood when the limo was lowered again, shooting Melinda a smile, her bright blue eyes filled with wry humor. ''Just like a man, isn't it? He needs fixing but won't admit he has a problem, and won't accept any help.''

Chuckling, Melinda got into the limo on the passenger side while Natalie slid behind the wheel. ''Do you have time to take me up to the ranch and then back to Paul's? I've got to work on payroll and month-end reports.''

Natalie backed the limo out of the stall, easing it around toward the driveway. ''No problem. Both the kids are at a friend's house all afternoon.''

''Your boy's healthy now?''

''Andy's fine. He just doesn't like to hang around the house when Rocky is at home, particularly if his dad is drinking. Neither do I, for that matter.''

''I gather from your earlier comment that Rocky doesn't want to get fixed.''

''He refused to go to the counselor, and he's being really nasty about everything the children or I do. I think he's getting ready to file for divorce.''

Melinda shuddered, not wishing that trauma on her friend, even if it had been coming for a long time. ''You better make copies of all your financial records. Orly did nothing but lie about how little money he made and what my assets were.''

''I don't even know where to begin.''

''The tax returns and pay stubs, if you can find them.''

Natalie nodded but didn't speak, watching for traffic.

Placing her hand on her friend's arm, Melinda gave a squeeze. ''I'm sorry your marriage is falling apart.''

''I feel like such a failure.''

Melinda could understand that. Even though she and Orly had grown apart long before the divorce, she'd foolishly fought as hard as she could to keep the marriage together. Her parents had been happily married for almost fifty years. It didn't seem right that her vows hadn't lasted ten.

But then, Hamilton Dumas had never been unfaithful to his wife—or left her nearly destitute, aided and abetted by a skilled attorney.

Paul knew now that Orly had lied to him. But that didn't mean he'd take his own client back to court to rectify the unjust settlement.

They reached the turnoff to the ranch, and Natalie expertly maneuvered the limo up the winding road to the ranch house, pulling to a stop in front of the porch. Melinda was grateful that her friend's distraction about her own failing marriage meant she hadn't asked any questions about Paul, or why Melinda was living at his house. She wasn't sure she could have answered them honestly, even to herself.

"It will take me just a minute to get what I need," she told Natalie. "Come on in, if you'd like."

"That's okay." Getting out of the limo, Natalie leaned against the fender and inhaled deeply. "The pine trees smell wonderful. I'll stay here and breathe the fresh air while I wait."

Amused by her friend's sudden desire for the great outdoors, Melinda went inside.

Compared with Paul's home, the empty house seemed dark, the furniture heavy and forbidding, the stale air oppressive, without life or light.

It hadn't been that way when Jenny was alive. Then it had been a home filled with love, with knickknacks and photos scattered about, bringing with them memories of family. In Zane's grief, he'd hidden away the mementos of the years he'd had with Jenny.

That's all Melinda had ever wanted—a home and family, a man to love who'd give his love to her in return. But the remnants of her own home, those she'd wanted to save after the divorce, were stored in crates and boxes in one of the horse barns, leaving her with a vague sense of rootlessness.

As she got her laptop and the papers she'd need, her thoughts slipped irresistibly to Paul. He was the perfect family man—his brother and sisters, nieces and nephews and his mother all recipients of his love. And they returned his love in kind.

To Melinda, he'd been a thoughtful friend—amazingly so, considering they'd been on opposing sides of a court battle. And he was attracted to her. She wouldn't deny she was tempted by him, too.

Her chest tightened and her heart began to beat erratically at the possibility that, however much she had resisted the idea, he might be the answer to her lifelong dreams.

Her promised two-week stay hadn't run out yet. A few more days at his house—just while her limo remained in the body shop, she rationalized—would be worth it.

But would it be worth the risk to herself and her children to succumb to the lure of another knight, this one driving a silver-gray Mercedes?

A man who made it clear that wedding vows were not part of his life's plan?

CHAPTER EIGHT

FIGHTING THE TEMPTATION to walk right in and hopefully catch Melinda in her nightgown again, Paul rapped on her bedroom door. He'd gotten home late from the office, missed dinner and hadn't bothered to change clothes yet. But he was anxious to see her.

After a moment's pause, she called, "Come in."

He opened the door in time to catch a glimpse of her hands moving away from her neck brace, which she'd no doubt put on *after* he knocked. He stifled a smile. He really ought to tell her she didn't need to keep up the charade of being injured, but he preferred that she tell him herself.

Idly, he wondered if she'd contacted an attorney yet, and hoped not. Surely she could see by now that he didn't deserve her ire. And he was trying to rectify the errors in judgment he'd made.

"What was the verdict on the second limo?" he asked.

She presented an enticing picture sitting cross-legged in the middle of the bed, balancing a laptop on her knees, her hair mussed, a yellow pencil tucked behind her ear. There was a hint of innocence about her, mixed with overt sex appeal.

"Fortunately, Larry's chassis passed inspection."

"I'm sure Rutledge was relieved to find you didn't expect him to operate on a man named Larry."

A wry smile played across her lips and crinkled the corners of her eyes, making Paul wish he could shove aside all the papers and the computer and join her on the queen-size bed.

To prevent himself from doing just that, he slid his hands into his pockets. "I was thinking that we've skipped a couple of nights' reading. We're never going to finish that mystery if we don't stick with it." *Or if you keep avoiding me.*

"I've really got to get some work done tonight. I've got payroll taxes and month-end bills to pay."

"You're your own accountant?"

"Bookkeeper. The program I use does everything for me except paste the stamps on the envelopes."

"I'm impressed." He edged around to the side of the bed, peering with interest over her shoulder at the computer screen. "Did you take accounting in school?"

"A bookkeeping class in high school. My folks wanted me to go to college, and I did for a couple of semesters. But I much preferred working around the ranch, or being a wrangler on backpacking trips out of Tahoe in the summers." She glanced at the computer screen, which was filled with rows and columns of numbers. "As usual, Mom and Dad were right. I should have stuck with college."

"You could go back to school."

She looked up at him. "In my spare time, right?

As if, with two kids and a business to run, I have any.''

''It's all a question of priorities.'' His priority was to spend more time with Melinda, which wasn't going to happen if he let her hide out in her room during the few hours he was home in the evening.

''If you don't want me to read to you, come sit with me while I have dinner. You've got a couple of days till month end. You can work on that tomorrow.'' He nodded toward the papers surrounding her. ''And I'm sure Tilly put something away for me. It will taste much better if I have company.''

''There's a plate warming in the oven.''

''Great.'' He held out his hand to her. ''Nothing better than a dried-out dinner when you share it with a friend.''

Reluctantly, Melinda slipped her hand into his, experiencing the usual fluttering in her midsection. Just how much could she risk with Paul without losing herself? She didn't want to fail again in a relationship as she had with Orly. With Paul, she sensed breaking up—if they did manage to get together—would be ten times more painful than it had been with her former husband. Paul was simply too dynamic a man not to leave a hole in a woman's life and heart after he'd gone.

Furthermore, she wasn't interested in simply having an affair. She had her children to think about.

Setting her laptop aside, she swung her legs over the side of the bed. ''That's certainly an invitation no woman could resist.''

''I'm a very persuasive guy. It's all in the technique. You have to start slow if you want to build to a really knock-your-socks-off climax. Gets to women every time.''

Her brows shot up. ''I wouldn't think of questioning your technique.'' Based on the one kiss they had shared, it was obviously quite skilled.

Without letting go of her hand, he led her downstairs, their fingers entwined, their thighs brushing. The contact sent heated messages to all of her nerve endings.

''How did the kids' day go?'' he asked.

''Fine. Tilly took them to a park she said was nearby.'' Melinda walked around the end of the serving counter into the kitchen, while he stayed on the other side, still holding her hand. She gazed at him curiously as his thumb sketched a path across her knuckles.

''That would be the fire engine park. In addition to the usual swings and slides, there's an old fire truck imbedded in the ground that the kids can climb on.''

''Ryan said something about that. He missed you at dinner.'' She'd missed him, too. His charming smile, his easy conversation both with her and her children. ''I let them stay up a little late, thinking you might get home. Tilly said you'd called saying you'd be late.'' Melinda was grateful for that; otherwise, she would have worried about him.

''I had to go back to the office after my court appearance. Paperwork tends to build up if I don't stay on top of it. I'll try to get away earlier tomorrow."

"All that work must make you hungry."

"Yes, it does." His voice had dropped to a low, husky tone that spread like warm syrup across her flesh and seeped into her pores.

"If you'll let go of my hand, I'll get your dinner out of the oven for you."

"I'd say my greatest hunger right now couldn't be satisfied by a plate of warmed-over stew."

Melinda swallowed hard and licked her lips, and his gaze followed the action of her tongue. "Tilly fixed chicken-and-rice casserole."

He tugged her back to his side of the counter, capturing her against his chest, trapping her arm behind her. "I can hardly wait to taste it."

Lowering his head, he covered her lips with his. She gasped in surprise, which allowed his tongue free access for a sensual journey of exploration in her mouth. He teased one side and then the other, his tongue dueling with hers in a passionate dance she'd all but forgotten.

Shifting position, he leaned back against the counter, holding her in the nest of his hips. Instinctively, she rubbed against his arousal, and a low groan escaped her throat. Or maybe Paul had uttered the deep, needy sound. She couldn't be sure. She only knew it echoed the feeling that throbbed low in her body.

She became a prisoner of her own desire, a captive of his determined seduction. Her mouth was wild under his as she sought release from heat as burning as the sun, as ethereal as the moon.

Except for the rasp of their breathing, the house was still. Tilly had gone to her room hours ago; the children slept upstairs, tired from a day of play. Melinda and Paul were alone.

She wanted him. Wanted to experience every bit of his skilled technique. The fevered pitch she knew he would arouse in her.

"Paul?" she whispered, almost a plea for him to take her now. On the kitchen floor, if need be.

"You taste delicious." He nibbled kisses along her jaw, beneath her ear. "A great recipe. Just the right amount of spice."

She started to laugh, but his tongue found her ear, circling the rim, and all she could do was moan in pleasure as gooseflesh tracked down her spine. "Oh, my..."

"Feels good, huh?"

"Mmm." More than good. Closer to ecstasy, giving a starving woman all that she craved.

His hand slipped up from her waist to cradle her breast. "I've wanted you ever since—"

The phone rang.

His hand froze in place, and she went rigid.

"Let it ring," he said, his hungry, dark eyes on her.

Her mind raced. The sleeping children. Tilly. "No, everyone will wake up." She reached for the extension on the counter. Unable to speak, barely able to draw a steady breath, she handed the instrument to Paul.

He fixed her with a look that spoke volumes about the interruption and what he intended to do when he hung up. ‘‘This better not be a telemarketer,’’ he muttered, taking the phone from her.

Before he put the instrument to his ear, Melinda heard feminine laughter, and a second later, Paul’s cordial greeting.

Jealously ripped through her, and she slipped out of his embrace. What woman would be calling at ten o’clock at night? Not one of his business associates, she was sure. A girlfriend? A former lover? Melinda couldn’t bear the thought.

Pulling open the sliding glass door, she stepped out onto the deck rather than eavesdrop on his conversation. She’d been fooling herself. With his obvious wealth, Paul must run with a fast crowd that undoubtedly included fast women. Sexy women with long legs, terrific figures and not a stretch mark in sight. Women who didn’t hold out for marriage.

She couldn’t compete with that. Not in looks. And most certainly not in the money department. She wasn’t even sure she could make the grade in bed, given the chance.

A chance she’d just blown by answering the damn phone!

PAUL FINISHED the conversation, cradled the phone and glanced outside. Melinda was mad. From the rigid set of her slender shoulders and her wide-legged stance, he guessed she was about to explode. Or tear into him.

He smiled to himself. Damned if she wasn't jealous.

Sliding the door open, he stepped outside. ''Sorry about the interruption.''

''Don't worry about me. I wouldn't want to interfere with your love life. I'll just go back upstairs and get some work—''

''I do believe you're jealous.''

She whirled toward him. ''Me? Jealous? In your dreams, DeMarco.''

Pleasant dreams, indeed. ''That was a business call.''

''Right. I heard her voice, Paul. Come-hither dripped from her lips with every word. You don't have to lie to me. I'm just a houseguest, remember? I've got no claim on—''

''She's a private investigator.'' Who had discovered that Orly Haas had made a substantial deposit to an offshore account only a month before the divorce papers had been filed. Obviously, Melinda hadn't known about the money. If Paul had any advice for women it would be that they needed to stay on top of the family finances. In the case of a divorce—or a spouse's death—the information was crucial.

But Paul didn't want to tell Melinda yet what he was doing for fear she'd get her hopes up and he wouldn't be able to force Orly back into court to change the settlement agreement. To make the change stick, Paul needed more information, which A.J. would get for him. Soon, he hoped.

"Her name is Adrian Jordan," he said. "Her husband's a cop and they have three kids. She used to be on the Reno force, too, and she's the best private eye in the state."

"Oh. I didn't know." The steam went out of Melinda's fury. Her shoulders relaxed, and the taut line of her lips softened, tempting him again.

"Divorce attorneys use private eyes regularly." Paul figured it was safe to get closer, resume the activity the phone call had so rudely interrupted. A.J. might be the best detective in the state, but her timing was rotten.

"It was only reasonable for me to think..." Melinda hesitated. "A man like you...you must have dozens of women who are interested."

"If it makes you feel any more comfortable, my last date was the Bar Association dance in April. I took an attorney whom I haven't seen outside the courthouse since. Before that, I went to a fund-raiser for public television. Between work and my family, my schedule is too full for much socializing." Using his fingertips, he brushed a stray lock of her hair back behind her ear. "Until recently, that is."

A visible shudder rippled through her. "I shouldn't have jumped to conclusions about you."

"Nope." Sensing he'd overcome her objections, he bent down to kiss her. "Now, where were we?"

When she didn't retreat, he tasted the sweetness of her lips again, a flavor a man could learn to crave.

He puzzled over why that was so. He'd known women who were more beautiful, more sophisticated. But none had intrigued him the way Melinda did. She made him hunger for her taste, yearn to caress her, no matter the time of day or night. She'd addicted him to the fresh scent of mint.

He eased them both down to the padded chaise longue beside the pool and stretched out, propping himself above her on his elbow. The slightest breeze rippled the water, catching the light from inside the house and refracting it like moon glow on the sides of the pool. His thoughts scattered in the same way as he slid his hand beneath her blouse and palmed her breast. A perfect fit. So was her mouth as he angled his head to enjoy the soft fullness of her lips.

He kneed her legs apart and stroked the smooth skin of her thighs, letting his hand wander to the apex. He could feel her heat even through the cotton fabric of her shorts.

''Paul!'' she gasped.

''Yes, I know.'' How good it felt to have her locked in his embrace. To hear her soft moans. To have her taste on his lips, her leg draped over his.

To have the damn phone ringing again! The shrill sound shattered the still night.

''We're not going to answer it.'' He ground out the words and kissed her to stifle any objection she might make. If A.J. had more news for him, it could wait until tomorrow. Or the next day, if he could manage to make love to Melinda that long.

As the phone rang a third time, he felt her ease away, her passion ebbing and wary tension returning.

"You're sure that isn't an old girlfriend checking up on you?" she teased in a whisper.

"If it is, she's set on becoming past tense." He rested his forehead against Melinda's and breathed deeply, the phone now silent. "How about continuing this upstairs—after I unplug every damn phone in the house?"

Her ripple of laughter curled into his chest. "I think somebody must be trying to tell us this is a bad idea."

"Impossible. All of my ideas are superior. Particularly this one." He dipped his head—

"Mr. D! Mr. D!" Tilly came racing out onto the deck, her gray hair in disarray, her chenille bathrobe open and fuzzy slippers flapping on the concrete. "It's your sister Angela! She's on her way to the hospital! She's having the baby!"

Muttering a mild curse, Paul struggled to his feet and helped Melinda up, blocking Tilly from having a clear view of what they'd been up to.

Timing was everything, and tonight his had been completely out of sync.

EXCEPT FOR THE CHILDREN, the entire DeMarco clan had put in an appearance at the hospital by the time Paul and Melinda showed up. Prospective aunts and uncles filled the chairs in the waiting area and overflowed into the hallway.

Melinda felt uncomfortable, out of place. She

wasn't part of the family, but Paul had insisted she come along, as though he didn't want to let her out of his sight.

As though he had plans for her later tonight.

She shivered at the memory of him holding her, kissing her. And the desire that had filled her until she ached with it. Surely it was just as well they'd been interrupted, because there was no way she would have found the willpower to stop.

And then how on earth could she even consider suing the man?

"Where's Max?" Paul asked, referring to the father-to-be.

"In with Angela, where else?" Olivia answered, standing on tiptoe to kiss Paul's cheek. "Mama's in there, too."

"Has he fainted yet?"

They all laughed; apparently it was a family joke.

"Not so far," Carl responded. "But we keep listening for a code blue."

In an aside to Melinda, Paul said, "Max faints at the sight of blood. He managed to pass out at the critical moment with both of their kids. He's been practicing deep-breathing exercises for the past eight months."

"And Angela's been practicing resuscitation," Olivia added, to the general laughter of all.

Melinda laughed with the family. She remembered Zane and Zach coming to the hospital for Nancy's delivery. No matter that she was very fond of her brothers, she'd been a bit piqued at their reference to her as a heifer about to drop her calf. She supposed ranchers had a different view of the birthing process.

In truth, her pregnancies and deliveries had gone exceptionally well. The doctor said she was made for making babies. Had her husband been anyone but Orly, she'd have happily expanded her family to three or four children. But by the time Ryan came on the scene, she'd already suspected she'd made a dreadful mistake marrying Orly.

The maternity waiting area ebbed and flowed with assorted family members wandering off for soft drinks or coffee, candy bars and apples. When the door to the inner sanctum opened, they all stood like marionettes on a single set of strings.

Max, looking as pale as a bleached white sheet, appeared with Paul's mother. The two-hundred-pounder leaned heavily on his mother-in-law's arm.

"Not yet," Mrs. DeMarco announced to the entourage. "Max just needed a break."

Everyone groaned in disappointment and resumed their earlier positions.

Olivia's husband, Nick, hooked his arm around Max's waist. "Come on, buddy. Let's get you something cool to drink."

"Oh, Paul, I'm so glad you came," his mother exclaimed. Then she took Melinda's hands. "You, too, my dear."

"I don't feel like I belong here, Mrs. DeMarco. I don't want to intrude."

The older woman glanced at her eldest. "I suspect

you're exactly where you belong,'' she said softly. ''Or my son wouldn't have brought you.''

A rush of embarrassment and guilt brought heat to Melinda's cheeks.

Olivia grabbed Paul's arm. ''You and Melinda take a turn now sitting with Angela. We don't want to leave her alone.''

''Forget there's a medical staff of hundreds at her beck and call,'' he said wryly.

''Hush!'' his sister said, chastising him. ''They're not family!''

That was the crux of the matter, Melinda thought, when Paul dragged her into the labor room. She *wasn't* family. But as soon as she saw Angela propped up in bed, her dark hair lanky with sweat, it no longer mattered. Melinda recalled all too well the fear, if not the pain, of labor. She took her hand.

''Thanks for coming,'' Angela said. She glanced at her brother. ''You, too.''

''I'm getting to be an old hand at this uncle business. How are you doing?''

''More to the point, how's Max?''

''Nick's got him under his wing.''

She smiled softly, then grimaced as another contraction hit her. ''Poor guy.''

Melinda pulled up a nearby stool, sitting down next to the expectant mother and holding her hand. As Paul and his sister talked, she watched the rhythmic peaks and valleys caused by the baby's heartbeat on the overhead monitor. A child. A new baby to be loved and spoiled by the extended DeMarco family. Lucky kid.

Lucky the woman who could be a part of that family.

She frowned suddenly, noting that the rhythmic beats on the monitor had changed dramatically, as though the baby's heartbeat was in distress. ''Paul!''

Before he could respond, the door flew open and both a nurse and a doctor appeared.

''You want to see if you can get the daddy in here?'' the nurse requested, even as she was maneuvering Angela to her side.

''What's wrong?'' Paul asked, panic in his voice.

Melinda took his arm. ''Come on, Paul. They've got work to do and we need to get Max back in here.''

After that, time seemed to drag. Muted voices drifted out to the waiting area from the labor room—the doctor giving instructions; Max issuing encouragement, punctuated by an occasional well-placed curse from Angela as she labored to deliver her child.

Paul paced. Olivia tried to doze in an upholstered chair. Sitting nearby, Melinda remembered the birth of her own children, and struggled with her conscience.

''What's taking so damn long?'' Paul muttered.

Melinda held out her hand to him. ''It doesn't sound like there's a problem. The baby's just taking its own sweet time about arriving.''

''Well, she ought to get on out here. I've got a

giant stuffed Saint Bernard at home in the closet waiting for her.''

Smiling, she squeezed his hand. ''It's a girl?''

''Angela said she was trying to even up the ratio of boys and girls.''

At that moment, a baby cried in the adjacent room. Healthy and hearty, and mad as hell.

Tears swam in Melinda's eyes and her throat constricted. Paul pulled her to her feet and drew her close as she felt an incredible surge of love overwhelmed her—a maternal instinct for the newborn and something even more elemental for the man who held her.

''Thank God,'' he murmured.

Within twenty minutes, a nurse appeared carrying a tiny infant wrapped tightly in a blanket, a pink knitted cap on her head.

''Our new mom and dad wanted me to introduce Pauline Marie to her family, especially to her uncle Paul,'' the nurse said.

''Pauline?'' Paul's voice caught.

She held out the baby to him.

As though he had a dozen children of his own, Paul took his baby niece into his arms, holding her snugly. Unabashedly, he let tears roll down his cheeks.

''Welcome to the family, Pauline,'' he whispered.

Stunned by the depth of his emotion, Melinda fought her own tears and lost the battle, along with everyone else in the room, the nurse included. Paul was such a kind, loving man. How could Melinda not love him, too? Yet how could she justify the impact his career and hard-driving ambition had on innocent victims of divorce?

Her heart felt torn and ragged, as if split down the middle. A part of her wanted to give him a baby of his own with chocolate-brown eyes and a sweet smile.

Another part warned that falling in love with a man who had no use for matrimony would be disastrous.

Olivia regained her composure first and snapped a picture of Paul and the baby. Soon the others took turns at holding the baby, cooing foolishly as adults do with infants.

Over a good many objections, the nurse retrieved the newborn from her aunts and uncles, who then visited the weary parents. Angela glowed. Poor Max, big man that he was, looked as if he'd been through a fifteen-round boxing match—and lost.

By the time Melinda and Paul got home, dawn was just beginning to lighten the eastern sky. They went upstairs quietly. To Melinda's surprise, Paul caught her hand before she reached the door to her room.

"It seems to me you and I have some unfinished business," he said, his voice low and husky.

CHAPTER NINE

SHE DIDN'T PLAY COY. She knew exactly what he was talking about.

A mix of adrenaline and leftover caffeine from the hospital coffee surged through her veins, along with deeper emotions. The swell of love she'd felt for Paul as he'd held his baby niece. Her unruly desire to be the woman who could give him a child of his own, the woman he could love.

Still she hesitated, her mind leapfrogging through a thousand reasons why she shouldn't agree to what her heart cried out to do.

"It's late," she whispered. "The children—"

"They'll sleep for another two hours at least. Maybe more." He linked his fingers with hers, tugging her closer. "We have time."

"I don't want you to think—"

"All I'm thinking now is that I want you, and this time nothing is going to interrupt us short of the house burning down."

"You know, my neck is about as good as it's going to get. I really think tomorrow the children and I ought to leave." She needed to stop lying to him, stop taking advantage of his kindness. Risking a heartbreak she wasn't sure she'd survive.

"I don't want you to go." With that he emphatically made his case, lifting her in his arms and carrying her into his bedroom. With his foot, he closed the door behind them. His dark, burning eyes caught and held hers, and she was the one on fire.

The bed in his room was much larger than hers, a giant king-size with three pillows, the quilt covering in deep masculine tones of burgundy and forest green. With one hand, he tossed the bedding aside, lowering her until the cool sheets felt chill against her back even through the fabric of her blouse.

"I can't tell you how long I've wanted you here...with me," he murmured.

His skillful fingers plucked at the buttons on her shirt at the same time that his mouth devoured hers with teasing, nipping kisses. Deep, hungry kisses. Then his lips touched the skin he'd exposed, brushing lightly before his tongue licked new flames across her flesh.

She groaned, wanting to feel more. Needing to experience all he had to offer. The low sound she made was as sensual as any she'd ever uttered. Embarrassing in the way it demanded more of him. Of her.

Tugging her blouse from her waistband to reveal her skimpy bra, he sighed as though he'd found the treasure he'd been searching for.

"Silk?" he asked, his mouth covering her peaked nipple.

"Mmm."

"Your undies, too?"

"Yes...I think..." His hand slipped beneath the waistband of her slacks, where he found her hot and slick with wanting. "Paul, I—"

"Let's see if you still object to my technique." His broad hand covered her mound, and she cried out.

"Mel, Mel, you feel so good."

She squirmed, trying to find a way to ease the throbbing ache. Desperately she ripped off the confining neck brace that had imprisoned her for too long, and in the next instant his lips were soothing the itch that had driven her crazy, teasing along the column of her throat. Her skin had never been more sensitive, more eager for a man's caress. Paul's caress.

Her fingers worked free the buttons on his shirt, and he helped her by shrugging out of it, then tossing it aside.

She palmed his chest, free for the first time to run her fingers through the fine mat of dark hair, to give in to her urge to explore his rippling muscles. To feel the heat of him.

Her mouth was wild under his. Greedy. Avid to devour him. His taste was salty and male, coffee flavored; his tongue was both velvety and rough.

She toed off her shoes, letting them drop to the carpeted floor with a soft plop. Paul tugged off her slacks, leaving her panties in place.

"Hot red silk," he murmured. "Perfect."

His mouth closed over silk, and she swallowed the scream that rose in her throat as she exploded beneath him. Sudden, unexpected, the orgasm slammed through her.

"Oh, my," she whispered. "I had no idea...."

"We're only beginning."

Limp with her release, she was barely aware of Paul, stripping her panties away and doing the same with her bra. And then he was naked, too, crushing her breasts to his chest, his arousal pressing against the apex of her thighs. The throb of need pulsed through her. She was on fire again. With each stroke of his hands on her breasts, her stomach, her legs, the flames flickered more brightly, blinding her.

She'd experienced sex before. Had enjoyed it to a point. But never had she imagined an encounter could be so all-consuming. Paul was giving her something only he could provide. Something far greater than simple physical pleasure.

Seeking the fulfillment he promised, she shifted beneath him and speared her fingers through the sensual fullness of his hair. As she drew him closer, she kissed his mouth, his cheeks—everywhere her lips could reach.

And still he denied her what she needed.

"Paul, please..." His mouth was on her breast now, sucking the nipple in, drawing hot, wet circles with his tongue. She climaxed again. Ripples of heat sped from her core outward to engulf her entire being, and she was seized by a knowledge as elemental as the universe.

There would never be another man for her. Only Paul.

"We're almost there," he whispered, brushing kisses on her sweat-dampened face. The taste of her sex was on his tongue, the scent of her filled his nostrils. Her glazed eyes were wide with wonder and ardor, and he eased away from her, reaching for the silver packet in the night table drawer. Ripping it open, he rolled the condom on.

"Stay with me," he urged, testing her slick readiness with his fingertips, then kneeing her legs apart. He moved between them, and with a quick thrust, buried himself within her heat.

For an instant he remained still, stunned by the pleasure of having her, and by the hot pulsing inside her.

His gaze locked with hers and he began to move. Slowly at first. Wanting to draw out the gratification. His and hers. He watched her pulse beat wildly at her throat, her breasts rising and falling with each thrust.

"Wrap your legs around me."

She did, locking herself to him, holding on while he increased the pace, rocking faster and faster. Her head tossed from side to side on the pillow, her hair damp. Her breath was coming in rapid gasps. Nothing had ever felt so good as the heated friction as he moved in and out of her. Nothing pleased him more than seeing her responding to him, utterly seduced.

"Look at me. I want to see you come."

"Paul, I—" Her eyes widened, dark and fully dilated, and he saw that exquisite moment of culmination burst through her.

He covered her mouth with his to swallow her cry, and sank even more deeply within her. She pulsed around him, squeezing him. Holding him with her arms and with her body. Drawing from him a cry that echoed her own pleasure.

Dazed by the power of his release, Paul could barely refrain from collapsing on her. With the last of his strength, he rolled to his side, pulling her with him. Moments later, their bodies still locked together, he drifted off to sleep.

MELINDA FLOATED in the afterglow of Paul's incredible lovemaking, warm and secure in his embrace. She felt boneless. Weightless.

And filled with guilt.

The false pretenses that had gotten her here, her faked injury, her appalling plan to sue him, now seemed vengeful and ugly. Unworthy of her and undeserved by Paul. Particularly when he had shown her—and her children—nothing but kindness and generosity.

It wasn't enough that she had told him her neck was fine now. She had to confess all, tell him the truth. And if need be, she would have to accept the consequences of her lie.

Lovingly, she stroked her hand across Paul's shoulder. The scent of his maleness mixed with the intimate perfume of her own well-sated body created a sensual fragrance that lingered in the air.

"Paul?" she whispered. "There's something I need to tell you. Please don't be angry."

His only response was the soft breathing of a man deep in sleep.

She smiled to herself. Tomorrow would be soon enough for her confession—or rather this morning, after they'd dozed awhile. Her own eyelids were too heavy now, her heart too full for a serious discussion. Later would do just fine.

Snuggling against the heat of his body, she closed her eyes.

''GOOD MORNING, sleepyhead,'' he whispered against her lips.

''Umm.'' With a smile, she opened her eyes and started. ''You're dressed!''

''I've got a nine o'clock appointment with a client. I want your promise you'll be here when I get back tonight.''

''Tonight?'' She struggled to sit up. ''But we need to talk—''

''You'll have my full attention when I get home.'' His lips curved in a satisfied masculine grin. ''My *full* attention, I promise.''

''No, you don't understand. I have to tell you—''

He silenced her with a kiss. ''Promise me you'll be here?''

''Well, yes, I guess...'' She couldn't simply leave without telling him why, without apologizing and assuring him she no longer planned to sue. That she was hoping they would have a future together.

Obviously pleased with her promise, he winked at her—which sent tingles down her spine—then marched out the door, whistling a tuneless song. A contented man.

With a groan, Melinda fell back on the pillow. A self-satisfied smile lifted her lips. Explanations could wait. For now, she planned to immerse herself in the memories of last night.

The next thing she knew, Nancy was calling her.

"Mom! Where are you?"

Flying out of bed, Melinda grabbed up her clothing, which Paul had thoughtfully laid out at the foot of the bed, and raced into the adjoining bathroom.

"I'm in here, dear," she called breathlessly, cracking open the door to her bedroom an inch. "I was about to take my shower."

"Can we go see Aunt Angela's baby today? Tilly says it's a girl."

"We'll see. I'll be out in a couple of minutes, and we'll talk then." Closing the door, she rested her forehead against it. No way was she ready to explain to her daughter how she happened to be in Paul's bed. Naked. The child already had too much matchmaking on her mind. And Melinda wasn't entirely sure where she'd stand with Paul once she confessed her lie.

Although, if she had her way, *standing* wasn't the position of choice.

She glanced at the inviting Jacuzzi and smiled. That household amenity offered all sorts of possibilities.

FOR A MAN WHO'D HAD a scant two hours of sleep, Paul felt damn good as he stepped off the elevator.

That's what great sex did for him, and it had never been better than last night. He was already looking forward to the end of the day.

If his appointments allowed, maybe he'd catch a catnap. He hoped Melinda would be able to do the same. He wanted them both to be wide awake and ready.

He saluted his receptionist with a cheerful wave. "Good morning, Stacy."

"Good morning, Mr. DeMarco. Olivia called with the news. Congratulations on your new niece."

"She's a real winner. Can't decide if I want her to grow up to be Miss Universe or the president of the United States."

"Why not both?" Stacy suggested.

"Good idea." Chuckling, he headed down the hallway to his office. He'd been incredibly touched to have Angela and her husband name their baby after him. For a man who had never considered himself a candidate for marriage, it gave him a sense of continuity. Naturally, he loved all his nephews and his niece, but little Pauline was going to be something special. He could feel it in his bones.

He had just enough time to look over his messages before Myrna let him know his new client had arrived in the reception area. Paul asked her to show him in.

With luck, he'd be able to make quick work of this interview, clear off his desk early and get back home before dinner. After years of being a workaholic, he felt it was time to back off and enjoy life a little.

With Melinda, if he had his way.

"THE CHILDREN ABSOLUTELY insisted on seeing the baby." Melinda added her bouquet of cut flowers to a room already overflowing with floral arrangements. The DeMarco family certainly knew how to celebrate the birth of a baby. "I hope you don't mind. I told them we can't stay long."

"It's fine, really." Looking radiant, considering she'd given birth less than twelve hours ago, Angela smiled at her visitors. "Max is going to bring Tony and Victor by later on this afternoon to meet their sister. After he catches up on his sleep, I imagine."

Tilly, who had driven Melinda and her children to the hospital, edged up to the bed to get a better look at the baby in Angela's arms.

"Oh, isn't she a pretty thing. And so much hair, too. I remember when—" Her voice caught, and Melinda knew the older woman must be thinking of the child she'd lost. "Precious baby."

Ryan peered over the bed railing and frowned. "Mom, if you make another baby, could you make it a boy? One sister is all I need."

Melinda wasn't sure how to respond to her son's request.

"You could have twins," Nancy suggested. "Like Uncle Zane and Uncle Zach, except one of each kind."

"You two have forgotten a few little details," Melinda told her children. ''We'd need to have a daddy around before there's any chance of me having either a brother or a sister for you.''

Angela's amused gaze met hers. ''How *is* Uncle Paul this morning?''

A guilty flush burned Melinda's cheeks. ''Fine. Very pleased to have the baby named after him, I think.''

''He's been both father and brother to us for almost as long as I can remember, so it seemed the right thing to do. Particularly since there doesn't seem to be a junior in his future. Unless things have changed recently...'' Angela left the thought dangling in the air.

Melinda ignored it. ''I promised the kids I'd take them to McDonald's for lunch, and I have to make a stop at a drugstore somewhere.'' She hooked her hand over Ryan's shoulder. ''Not to mention you need to get some rest, Angela. So we'd better be going.''

Her children's comments and Angela's question had cut a little too close. Everyone, including Paul, had made it clear he had no intention of marrying. Of course, avowed bachelors could change their minds. But Paul wasn't the sort who vacillated. If he said marriage was out of the question, he probably meant it.

That left Melinda in the impossible position of trying to persuade a man who was capable of swaying both judge and jury to change his mind.

After she said goodbye to Angela, she ushered

Tilly and the children out of the hospital with the promise of lunch.

That afternoon, using the supplies she'd picked up at the drugstore, she primped and fussed over herself in a way she hadn't since her high school senior prom. She soaked in a tub of bath oil. Doused herself in skin cream. Shaved her legs. Did her nails. Used cucumbers to rid herself of the faint bags under her eyes, a residual of her mostly sleepless night.

If there'd been any possibility of success, she would have worked on losing ten pounds, too.

He arrived home in time for dinner, still whistling that same silly two-note tune.

''Hi, kids,'' he called to the children, who were perched in front of the TV. For Melinda, he had an intimate, for-her-eyes-only look that sent butterflies reeling in her already fluttering stomach. ''I brought ice cream for dessert.''

''What kind?'' Nancy asked, distracted from the cartoon show.

''Chocolate peppermint.''

''Yum!'' She hopped up and ran over to give Paul a hug.

With his free arm, he hugged her back. ''And Saturday, if your mom says it's okay, we're all going to fly to South Tahoe and ride the sight-seeing boat around the lake. Michael and Steven are coming, too. How's that sound?''

''Me, too?'' Ryan asked, the promise of an airplane ride finally drawing him away from the TV.

''You, too, champ.''

Cheering, Nancy jumped up and down. ''Can we, Mom? Can we?''

''Of course we can.'' Standing in the dining room, silverware in hand to set the table, Melinda blinked back tears, and her heart squeezed tight. Surely Paul realized what a good father he'd be, what a perfect husband. He already had the corner on being the perfect lover.

Relinquishing his hold on Nancy, he walked into the dining room. Surreptitiously, he slid his hand into Melinda's, his fingers cold from carrying the ice cream.

''You're a nice man, Mr. DeMarco,'' she said.

''In your case, I'm highly motivated.''

Feeling her cheeks flush, she asked, ''How did you know chocolate peppermint is my favorite?''

''I called your mother.''

''How sweet.'' She couldn't remember Orly ever doing anything as thoughtful. After ten years of marriage, she doubted he'd even noticed her favorite flavor of ice cream.

''I also got something for just the two of us,'' he said so softly only she could hear. ''For later.''

She lifted her brows. ''Oh?''

''Bubble bath for the Jacuzzi upstairs.''

''Oh, my...'' He must have read her mind. A perfect way to put the giant tub to use.

''All day I've been imagining you covered in bubbles and me blowing them off, up close and personal. It's been damn hard on my concentration as well as certain parts of my anatomy.''

Before Melinda could react, Tilly appeared out of the kitchen with a serving tray filled with bowls of shredded lettuce, chopped tomatoes, cheese and sizzling taco mix. ''Dinner's ready. Tacos and beans. Everybody come and get it.''

The children cheered.

Melinda groaned. Lordy, after Paul's announcement, eating was the last thing on her mind. She could barely finish setting the table her knees had gone so weak and her hands so shaky. All through dinner the only thing she could concentrate on was the image of her and Paul in the Jacuzzi, her legs wrapped around him as bubbles rose and he licked them off.

Oh, my…

''HOW LONG DO YOU THINK it will take them to get to sleep?'' he asked when she came downstairs to the family room after putting the children to bed. He stood, holding out his hand to her.

''I don't know. Ice cream might have been a bad idea. The sugar high won't speed things up.''

''A minor miscalculation.'' He pulled her to him, kissing her gently. ''I think I can wait. Briefly.''

She smiled against his lips. ''At least it will give me a chance to tell you something, make a confession of sorts.'' A biggie if he wasn't a forgiving man.

''If you're about to confess all of the men who've loved you in the past, I'm not interested.''

''Hardly. It wouldn't be a very long story, anyway.'' She chuckled and rested her head on his shoulder. Even after a day at work, his white dress shirt felt crisp beneath her cheek. "The problem is, I've lied to you and I'm really, really sorry I did."

"Lied?"

She lifted her head. "About the accident. I wasn't hurt, Paul. It was all an act. I faked my whiplash. I was so angry about the divorce settlement, and I blamed you. I was going to sue you."

"I know."

"I know it was childish of me. And vengeful. I want you to know I have no plans to—" Doing a mental double-take, she stopped midthought and backed up. "You knew?"

"Of course I knew you weren't hurt. I barely nudged your limo. And the nosedive you took wouldn't have qualified you for the novice division of any elementary-school acting class."

Stepping back, she planted her hands on his chest. "You knew I wasn't injured and you brought me here to recover?"

"I wanted us to have a chance—"

"You made me wear that damn neck brace for more than a week, and all the time—"

"I couldn't tell you. I was afraid you'd leave."

"You've got that straight! You brought me here under false pretenses."

"We'd been adversaries in the courtroom. I wanted to start over. Get to know each other."

"Why? Was all that phony kindness of yours—"

"I was attracted to you from the first time we met.

But I couldn't act. It wouldn't have been ethical, not when Orly was my client."

"Well, doesn't that just take the cake." Melinda sputtered from injured pride and humiliation. She'd been duped, for God's sake. Betrayed. Everything he'd done had been as much of a lie as her own behavior. She'd fallen for his line, hook and all. "Did you just want to get me into bed? Is that what this was all about? Wanting to hit on your client's ex-wife? Is that some kind of game you play? Is it? Your ultimate *win?*"

Her accusation shocked Paul. He opened his mouth to respond, to defend himself, and realized he couldn't speak. Was that what he'd been after from the beginning? To get Melinda into his bed?

How could he deny that he'd wanted her? In the courtroom. When she was lying on the sidewalk faking her injury. But it hadn't been a competition—a need to win. He could swear to that in a courtroom.

"Melinda—"

"No, don't say it. There have been enough lies between us." She backed away from him, holding her hands up as if to ward off evil. "If the children weren't already in bed, I'd pack them up right now and call a cab. But we'll leave in the morning. And there's nothing in the world you can say or do that will stop us."

"You promised to stay two weeks."

"Then sue me for changing my mind." With that, she whirled away and stormed up the stairs.

CHAPTER TEN

PAUL WALKED OUT onto the deck by the pool. Despite the placid turquoise water, the familiarity of everything around him, he felt as if he'd been punched in the gut.

Where the hell had the *sweet man* part gone?

Maybe he had brought her here under false pretenses. But his ploy hadn't been any worse than Melinda's phony whiplash story. She'd been planning to take him to court, damn it!

Lies. They'd both told them, at least by implication.

He didn't know how to go back and start over. How to undo what had happened between them. Some parts he didn't want to undo. Like holding her in his arms. Kissing her. Making love to her. Watching her come apart as she climaxed.

Pacing around the side of the pool to the shuffleboard court, he picked up the stick Ryan had no doubt left out and centered it on a disk. He gave a mighty shove. The disk went sailing past the end of the court, clipped a low retaining wall and flew off the edge into the night sky.

Damn! Served him right for losing his self-control.

The light from Melinda's window cut a yellow square in the concrete decking. She was upstairs packing. He could see her shadow moving back and forth across the square of light, and he didn't know how to stop her.

But he had to try to make his case. Persuasion was something he did well.

Back inside, he walked upstairs, stopping briefly at the door of the kids' room. The only sound was the sweet sleep of the innocent. His throat clogged at the realization of how much he'd miss them if Melinda took her family back to the ranch. Away from him.

He went into his bedroom, then into the bath, tapping on the adjoining door to Melinda's room. A strip of light beneath the door told him she was still up, but there was no answer to his knock.

''Melinda, let's talk. We can work this out.'' Negotiating was a skill he'd honed during his years of law practice. He'd be able to find common ground—if she'd give him a chance.

Gently, he tried turning the knob. It gave, and he pushed. Something was blocking the door. Probably her damn suitcase.

He wanted to curse. Or plead. Or force his way inside. But that wasn't his way. And when he got right down to it, he wasn't sure what he'd say. Only that he wanted her to stay.

At this point, he didn't think that would be a convincing argument.

BY MORNING, he still hadn't come up with any way to persuade Melissa to stay.

"But, Mom, why do we have to leave now?" Nancy complained.

"This is not our home, honey." Melinda handed her suitcase to the cab driver.

"Neither is Uncle Zane's ranch," Nancy persisted. "It's boring living there."

Dragging his suitcase behind him like an anchor, Ryan stumbled on the walkway. "We used to have our own house. How come we don't anymore?"

Paul felt his gut twist. It was his fault they were leaving—and his fault they didn't have a home of their own.

"Melinda, I'd like you to reconsider," he said. "You can stay—"

"No. My children and I appreciate your hospitality. Don't we, children?" she prodded.

Both youngsters nodded glumly.

"I would have driven you back to the ranch, if you'd asked."

"You have a busy schedule at the office, I'm sure." She held her head at a haughty angle, almost as though she were still wearing the neck brace. "The taxi will be fine."

Reluctantly, Paul pulled his wallet from his back pocket and dug out money for cab fare.

"That won't be necessary." Her eyes flashing with stubborn pride, Melinda wrapped her hand around his wrist, stopping him. Her fingernails were bare, the polish she'd worn for the past week wiped away. "We can take care of ourselves."

"Of course you can, but—"

She wasn't listening. She'd already climbed in the cab and slammed the door behind her.

Moments later, the taxi drove away, and Paul was left standing in front of his half-million-dollar house, the sun beating down on the decorative white-rock landscaping. He'd never felt quite so alone in his life, not even when he'd stood at his father's graveside and vowed he would never marry or have children.

He hadn't fully realized then just how much pain he'd been trying to save himself. Now he did.

JUST WHAT HE DIDN'T NEED on a morning like this was another new client. Myrna had ushered the man into his office then discreetly closed the door behind her, leaving them alone.

Extending his hand, he said, "Mr. Greene, I'm Paul DeMarco."

"Owen Greene, but my friends call me Rocky."

Paul could understand that. The man had big, beefy hands, rock-hard biceps and shoulders to match. Only his protruding stomach suggested he was letting himself go.

Gesturing toward the two chairs in front of his desk, Paul said, "Have a seat, Rocky, and tell me what I can do to help you."

"You can help me get rid of my witchy wife without it costing me an arm and a leg." When Rocky sat down, he made the visitor's chair look fragile.

Paul took his seat behind his desk and pulled a yellow pad from his desk drawer. ''Okay, let's start with some basic information.'' He ran through questions about Rocky's date of birth, where he'd been married and for how long. ''And your wife's name is?''

''Natalie. Used to be Natalie Wisdom. Now she's Natalie Stupid, as far as I'm concerned.''

Paul's pen froze in midstroke, and he looked up. ''Does your wife drive a limousine?''

''Yeah. Sometimes. She uses the money to buy the kids stuff like hundred-dollar sneakers, for God's sake. She'd be better off staying at home, if you ask me.''

Melinda's friend and driver. ''Tell me, Rocky, how does it happen you picked me for your attorney?''

''Hey, you represented my buddy Orly Haas. Did a hell of a good job. Cleaned his old lady's clock, if you know what I mean? And saved ol' Orly bundles by not askin' too many questions. You know, about his finances and stuff. I figure you'd be willing to do a little fudging for me, too.''

Paul winced. Evidently he was guilty of malpractice and should be taken to court himself. But he was going to make amends. The court order he'd worked so hard to achieve for Orly wouldn't stand long once he had a little chat with his former client. Both Paul and Orly would make it up to Melinda.

And he wasn't about to make the same mistake with Orly's buddy.

Shoving back his chair, Paul stood. "Mr. Greene, you and I have a serious conflict of interest. I can't ambulance chase, as it were, but I hope to God your wife asks me to represent her. Then we'll see whose clock gets scrubbed clean this time."

Rocky blanched, looking shell-shocked. "Now wait just one damn minute. You can't—"

"I suggest you leave now, Mr. Greene, if you don't want me to be a witness for your wife when your divorce case comes up in court. You've just admitted that you'd be willing to perjure yourself."

IN THE CENTER of the training ring, Melinda worked one of Zane's prize Arabian colts, snapping her long whip behind the horse's rump to keep him moving in a circle. It was two days since she'd returned to the ranch from Paul's house, and she felt as if she had more control over the untrained animal than she did over her own volatile emotions. The whip was not the only thing snapping. Her nerves were, too.

It was her own damn fault. She never should have faked a whiplash injury. Never should have moved in with Paul.

Never should have fallen in love.

In the heat of midday, sweat dripped down her cheeks, mixing with the tears she didn't want to shed, and she forced herself to concentrate on what she was doing. The dust rising from the colt's hooves. His steady pace. The way the animal worked hard, already displaying the floating gait and arched neck that had made his sire a champion.

She heard a truck drive up and glanced in that direction. Zach's pickup pulled to a stop near the horse barn and he got out.

Swallowing her tears, she wiped her face on her sleeve and eased the colt to a slower pace. She didn't want her brother's sympathy. Didn't want him to know what a fool she'd been.

"Hey, Zach, what's up?" she asked, proud of her casual tone.

"Not much." Tipping his Stetson to the back of his head, he stepped up on the lower rung of the corral fence, looping his arms over the top. "That's one good-looking horse, isn't he?"

"Zane knows how to breed the best." She let the colt come to a full stop, then hooked her arm around the animal's neck to give him a hug. "Good job, pretty boy. Good job."

"I finally got a letter from Zane. I called you at DeMarco's, but the housekeeper said you'd moved out." Zach climbed over the top railing and walked into the ring. "She seemed upset that you'd left. Is everything okay, sis?"

"Sure. It's fine."

"I thought maybe you and DeMarco were—"

"You thought wrong. What did Zane say in his letter?" she asked, unwilling to discuss Paul and their nonrelationship with her brother.

Zach frowned before pulling a slender envelope from his hip pocket. "Not much. He's in Argentina now, or he was when he mailed this. Says he's found some good breeding stock."

''Does he say when he's coming home?''

''Nope.'' He handed her the letter. ''The whole thing is pretty vague.''

Unfolding the plain sheet of stationery, she read the terse note in her brother's sprawling handwriting, then folded it again. ''At least he's alive. That's something.''

''Yeah. Something. I wish he'd at least called.''

''Me, too.'' She rested her hand on Zach's arm. The twins had always been close, standing shoulder-to-shoulder against the world when they were little boys, and she knew Zach had to miss his brother. ''He'll come home soon. I'm sure he will.'' She was less sure Zane would ever recover from his grief over the loss of his wife in such a dreadful car accident. ''Have you told Mom about the letter?''

''I was going over there now. I stopped by to see you first. See if anything was wrong.''

The colt nudged her in the back, bumping her, and she gave him a scratch under his jaw. ''Everything's hunky-dory here.''

''The kids?''

''They went with friends to the water park. They'll be back for dinner.''

''Well, then, if you're sure you're okay...''

''Right as rain.'' Assuming you counted a storm of daily tears good for a woman's health. ''Thanks for dropping by.''

''No problem. Wish we'd hear from Kerry, too, but wherever she is, she'd have to send up smoke signals, I suppose.''

"Guess the two of us will have to hold down the fort till our wanderlust siblings return. Tell Mom hi for me. I'll bring the kids by in a day or two to visit." When Melinda felt courageous enough to answer her mother's inevitable questions.

Zach seemed reluctant to leave. Finally, he told her goodbye, climbed over the rail fence again and walked to his truck.

She watched as the pickup rumbled back down the dirt track toward the main road. When it was out of sight, she turned to the colt, pulling him against her chest. The lump in her throat was so huge she thought she might choke on it.

"Melinda Dumas," she chided herself, "falling in love with Paul DeMarco has got to be the stupidest thing you've ever done in your entire life."

PAUL LISTENED to the ringing phone on the other end of the line, then the click of the answering machine and a male voice saying, "You've reached the Twin Bar Ranch, Zane Dumas speaking. I can't come to the phone right now. Leave a message."

Paul hung up. He was sick to death of hearing that guy's voice. He'd left a half-dozen messages for Melinda since she'd gone. All of them had been unanswered. No sense wasting the energy to leave another. She wasn't going to talk to him. Not on the phone, at any rate.

Flipping open the file on his desk, he sorted through the information A.J. had provided. She might have lost her figure after three kids, but she hadn't lost her edge in the detective business. Orly Haas was a scumbag of the worst kind. He'd lied to his wife. To Paul. And worse, to the court.

Hidden assets in an overseas account were only the beginning. A.J. had found an income stream from an undisclosed real estate partnership, and consulting fees to a phony corporation wholly owned by Orly. He was corporate president, treasurer and sole employee.

A muscle ticked in Paul's jaw. Perjury was not a crime judges ignored. It was an affront to the system—and their egos.

He punched the intercom button. "Myrna, I'd like you to get hold of Orly Haas for me. I'd like to see him in my office as soon as possible." Scrubbing his hand across his face, Paul wondered if setting things to right would get him back in Melinda's good graces. He sure as hell hoped so. "Tell Mr. Haas I think we can make some adjustments in his divorce settlement that would be to his benefit." Because if the man didn't agree to Paul's terms, the SOB would end up behind bars for perjury. Paul would see to it.

Even if it cost him his career.

"But he promised he'd take us flying," Nancy whined.

"I know, honey." Melinda tried to console her children. They'd both been up at dawn, so excited about a ride in Paul's airplane that they hadn't been able to sleep. They dressed and were waiting for Paul to show up at their door before the Saturday morning cartoons were over. It was barely nine o'clock. "But that was while we were staying at his house. I'm sure he didn't mean—"

"He's not like Dad," Ryan said, setting his jaw at a stubborn angle, not unlike her own. "He promised and he'll come."

"If he doesn't come," Melinda persisted, "it will be my fault. We had an argument. It wouldn't be fair to blame him." Why she was defending a man who had only wanted to get her into his bed was beyond her. Maybe it was guilt, because she'd wanted to be there, too. As many times as he was willing.

Folding her small arms across her chest like a schoolteacher about to reprimand a misbehaving student, Nancy jutted out her chin and glared at her mother. "He'll come. I know he will."

Melinda wasn't quite sure what to wish for. She didn't want to see Paul, much less be forced to endure his company. But she didn't want her children hurt, either. Orly had disappointed them too many times. They deserved better.

For the sake of their future, they needed to know men were capable of keeping a promise.

But in this case, she wasn't sure she wanted Paul to be the one to teach them that lesson. Not today. Not when her emotions were so raw.

"Mom! He's here!" Nancy went running for the front door and threw it open, bounding out onto the porch as Paul's Mercedes came to a stop.

"Told ya so," Ryan said, hurrying after his sister.

Closing her eyes, Melinda drew a steadying

breath. The effort did little to slow her galloping heart. *He'd kept his promise.* For the sake of the children, she told herself. It had nothing to do with her.

Moments later, one child tugging on each hand, they dragged him into the house, where Melinda stood rooted in place. She hadn't fixed her face and had barely brushed her hair. She was wearing her oldest jeans, since she hadn't planned to go any farther than the horse barns all day.

In contrast to her disheveled appearance, Paul looked gorgeous in a maroon-and-white-striped polo shirt with an open collar and khaki shorts, his dark hair slightly windblown from the drive up to the ranch.

His smile was hesitant as he came to a halt in front of her. "You ready to go?"

"No, I...I didn't think you'd come."

He slowly cocked one brow. "I always keep my promises."

Was that true? Maybe he kept his promises to his clients, but Melinda was afraid to trust him with her heart. They had deceived each other once. How could she have faith in his word now?

"Come on, Mom!" Nancy pleaded.

When she continued to stall, Paul looked sad and said, "If you've got other things to do today, I'll understand."

Both youngsters burst into a chorus of objections, on the verge of full-blown temper tantrums, which never happened. They were both usually so well behaved.

She couldn't be the one to disappoint her children this time. They'd endured enough setbacks in the past year. And she couldn't let them go flying without her. She'd worry and fret all day that the plane would crash. She'd never survive losing her children, and would rather die with them than be left behind.

Good grief, where on earth were these morbid thoughts coming from? Paul was a good pilot. She was sure of it. He did everything to perfection.

Including making love, she thought with a silent groan.

But she still wasn't willing for him to take her children off on his own.

"All right! All right! Hush now," she told the kids, giving Ryan a quick hug to quiet him. "Give me a minute to change clothes and then we can go. Should I fix us a lunch?" she asked Paul.

His smile was as pleased as the children's and did something fluttery to Melinda's midsection. Something she shouldn't allow to happen.

"No, we'll eat in South Tahoe, at a table overlooking the lake. I've made reservations."

She considered whether that was arrogance or wishful thinking on his part, and wasn't sure how to tell the difference.

An hour later her stomach was still unsettled as the plane lifted off from the airport east of town, with Paul at the controls, Melinda in the copilot's seat and four children in the back of the twin-engine plane.

Michael and Steven pretended to be old hands at flying, but they had as much trouble suppressing their excitement as Nancy and Ryan did.

The whining engines and the way the plane bounced around in the air did little to reassure Melinda that staying home might not have been a better course of action, temper tantrums notwithstanding.

"Seven-forty-sevens don't buck quite this much," she said as the earth dropped away below them. Buildings on the ground grew smaller as they headed out over the sparsely populated desert region near Reno.

"Hey, Mom, look how little the houses are," Nancy yelled over the sound of the engines.

Melinda didn't turn around. "Yes, dear. I see them."

Wearing wraparound dark glasses, Paul slanted her a glance and smiled. "The air will smooth out when we get a little higher."

"That would be good," she muttered. She wasn't afraid of flying, exactly, but she found being in a little plane a far different experience from traveling in an airliner. It was more intimate, since she was right next to the pilot, which made her feel vulnerable in a number of ways. Not all of them related to crashing to the desert floor.

Paul spoke into a hand-held microphone, and an unintelligible voice responded over the loudspeaker. He banked the plane toward the mountains, which made Melinda grab the armrest ever more tightly.

Next to her, Paul laughed. "Welcome to White Knuckle Airlines."

"Oh, you..." She swatted him with her hand, but his joke had relaxed her. Marginally.

When he leveled the plane's wings, he said, "You want to try flying it for a while? All you have to do is keep the nose pointed at that peak over there."

"No, not me," she said adamantly.

Nancy stuck her head between the front seats. "I do. Can I fly—"

Melinda whipped around to face her daughter. "You get yourself back in your chair, young lady, and buckle up. Nobody's flying this plane but Paul."

A scowl darkened the child's face. "Paul would let me."

"Sorry, kiddo." He patted Nancy's cheek. "You're not quite old enough and your legs aren't long enough yet. But when you're ready, I'd be happy to give you lessons."

Somewhat mollified, Nancy slipped back into her seat, only to be teased by Michael that he'd get his pilot's license years before she'd be old enough to fly.

The familiar childish bickering—and the smoother ride—managed to ease Melinda's fears. She looked out the window, trying to pick out landmarks. Highway 395 appeared as a narrow strip of black concrete, but she couldn't locate the road that led to the Twin Bar Ranch, and could barely spot a house or two nestled on the eastern slope of the Sierras. Everything looked so different from this altitude. If they had to make a forced landing she wouldn't have a clue where they were.

Until they passed the summit and Lake Tahoe came into view.

"Look, kids," she called out to them. "The lake." Blue and crystal clear despite dire warnings about pollution, the water reflected the surrounding mountains. Little wonder environmentalists considered the lake a national treasure.

Her heart stuttered briefly. "It's lovely," she whispered, almost to herself.

Paul heard her and covered her hand with his. "I'm glad you came along. I wanted you to see this."

The warmth of his palm felt so good, so reassuring. But she didn't want to relinquish the hurt and anger she'd felt at his betrayal. The way he'd led her on. Right into his bed. A part of her felt so damn used, even if she had been as eager as he.

She slipped her hand from beneath his. "This is a special treat for Nancy and Ryan. I'm sure they'll never forget it."

AFTER CIRCLING THE LAKE, Paul lined the plane up for the final descent into South Tahoe. The air density at this hour was still good, and landing wouldn't be a problem, despite the mile-high altitude.

He dropped the plane onto the runway with barely a bump and smiled to himself. Yeah, he wanted to impress Melinda. And the kids, of course. But mostly

Melinda. There had to be some way to get through to her. A way to start over.

He'd arranged for a rental SUV to be waiting for them. Piling the whole crew inside, he drove the lakeshore highway to the restaurant he'd picked out for lunch. But with four kids around, he didn't have much chance to talk with Melinda. Not privately, at any rate. And she was obviously on edge, using the kids as a buffer to avoid conversation with him.

He finally caught her alone on the sight-seeing boat. With the kids occupied by the scenery, she was standing at the railing, gazing down into the water. As the boat chugged across the calm lake, a breeze ruffled her hair, tossing the light brown strands into disarray.

He stood beside her, wanting to touch her, to smooth her hair into place, to hold her, but he was afraid to. "I was considering putting the kids over the side in a rowboat so we'd have a chance to talk."

She glanced up, a faint smile playing at the corners of her lips. With the sun so bright, her pupils were tiny black spots in a circle of brown sugar. So sweet yet so sad.

"They'd probably love it. Though I'm not too sure how skilled they'd be at rowing."

"That's part of my plan. I figure they'd go in circles for hours." Leaning back against the railing, he looked at her. Not the scenery or the other tourists milling around the deck. Only Melinda. He'd missed her so damn much.

She glanced away, toward the shoreline. "The

lake has always been one of my favorite places to visit. Thank you for bringing the children.''

''I didn't do it just for the kids.'' The ache in his throat was so painful, he spoke barely above a whisper. ''I wanted a chance to apologize to you. You didn't return my phone calls.''

For a long time she didn't respond, instead watching the V of waves spread out behind them and rock a passing motorboat. ''I shouldn't have lied to you, either. I'm sorry.''

''If I'd been an honorable man, I would have approached you directly. Asked you out when enough time had passed since the divorce. But then the accident happened.'' He lifted his shoulders in a helpless shrug. ''It seemed like too good an opportunity to pass up.''

''Because you knew I couldn't say no to your offer to be a knight in shining armor without risking your discovery of my lie?''

''You should have been a lawyer, Melinda. You're very good at cross-examination.'' At making him feel guilty, too. But he supposed, in a way, he deserved it.

She laughed, a humorless sound. ''I don't think so. I couldn't compete with someone like you. Someone who has to win no matter who gets hurt.''

''That's how the adversarial system works.'' He'd spent years in school, years practicing his craft, to best represent his clients' interests. She had to see the merit in that.

''Is it? Is it your job to zealously pursue the interests of your client to the detriment of all others?'' She looked up at him, her forehead furrowed.

''I made a mistake in your case. Or rather, Orly lied to me and I didn't check things out. I should have. I'm trying to rectify the problem.''

''That would be nice,'' she conceded, although she didn't appear overjoyed at the possibility or confident anything would change.

''I was hoping, well, that we could start over. You know, maybe go out a couple of times. Dinner. Dancing. Flowers. Candy.'' Whatever it took, he'd give it a shot.

''I don't think so, Paul. You're so far out of my league, and your way of thinking is so different from mine. I don't see much point in pursuing a relationship.''

Panic rocketed through him. ''We were good together.''

She closed her eyes, as though unwilling to let him see her thoughts. ''I know. But I need more than that.''

What? he wanted to ask. He'd give it to her if he could. But he wasn't used to groveling. His pride wouldn't let him beg. He'd worked too hard for all he'd achieved to be willing to give it up now. He had his responsibilities, a family that counted on him.

Damn, if she couldn't see that…

He felt the pressure of loss closing in on him. He was used to winning, damn it!

He didn't know how to deal with the tables being turned on him.

CHAPTER ELEVEN

MELINDA PULLED the last item—a snare drum—out of the trunk of the limo and put it on the skycap's trolley to be hauled to baggage check-in. It was 3:00 a.m. The rock group she'd transported from Harrah's had finished their gig and were due to perform in Atlanta tonight.

After six trips to the Reno airport since morning, hefting all their luggage, she felt like she'd been flying twenty-fours straight without benefit of an airplane. Her body ached clear to her bones.

She'd felt that way since she'd told Paul goodbye nearly a week ago.

The group's manager, a guy wearing scruffy jeans and an equally unkempt ponytail, signed the charge slip, adding a nice tip for her.

"Thanks, sweet cheeks. We'll see you next time we're in town."

"I'll be here." She had nowhere else to go, no way to get out of debt or support her children without working as long and hard as she could. No rescue in sight.

Parked behind her, Natalie had dislodged her half of the rock group, along with their mounds of luggage. When everything was sorted out, she walked up to Melinda's limo.

"I'm going to call it a night," Natalie said. "How 'bout you?"

"That's the last run as far as I know." Some days were like this, going a million miles an hour, then not a single pickup was scheduled for the next two days. Tomorrow she'd take the kids to visit her parents, something she tried to do once a week or so, then maybe she'd park the limo at the airport in the hope of catching a fare.

Removing her chauffeur's cap, Natalie ran her fingers through her short, blond hair. "I've decided to go ahead and file for divorce. I think Rocky's already seen an attorney."

"Oh, I'm sorry, hon."

"Yeah. Whatever. I thought maybe you could recommend somebody. A good attorney, I mean."

Melinda hesitated, then said, "Paul DeMarco is the best in the state." Whatever else she might think of the man, she'd rather he was working *for* Natalie than against her.

"The guy who filled in driving for you? The one you were living with?"

"That's the one."

"Say, how are you and he—"

"We're not."

"Oh." Natalie looked surprised. "He seemed real nice, and a hunk, too."

Forcefully, Melinda blocked the image of said hunk from her mind, particularly the picture of him naked in bed with her. "He'll get all he can out of Rocky, I can promise you that."

"Okay, I'll give him a call."

MELINDA SLEPT LATE the next day and didn't get to her mother's place until after lunch. Her father was napping on the couch, a pile of morning newspapers on his lap, when she arrived. Blinking awake, he came to his feet.

"Hi, Dad." She kissed his cheek and gave him a hug. He was a tall, slender man, his face weathered by years in the saddle as a rancher. As always, he wore jeans and a plaid cotton shirt with the sleeves rolled up. "How are you feeling these days?"

"Doing my best to keep up with your mother." He turned from Melinda to give Nancy and Ryan a welcoming hug. "And here are my two favorite grandkids."

"How come you always say that, Grandpa?" Nancy asked. "What about Keith and Kenny? Aren't they your favorites, too?"

"They're my favorite *twin* grandkids." He tweaked the tip of her nose. "And you're getting too smart for me, little miss."

Giggling, Nancy gave her grandfather another hug.

"Where's Mom?" Melinda asked.

"Shuffleboard court. Practicing, I suspect. There's a tournament next weekend."

"Can we go over there and watch, Mom?" Ryan asked.

"Sure, honey. I'll visit with Grandpa for a while and then come find you." The senior citizens' community, with its guard at the front gate, was a safe place for both the older residents and their visitors, even young children—as long as they behaved themselves. Melinda had no fears about letting Nancy and Ryan go to the recreation center by themselves. There were dozens of grandmas around to watch out for them.

Ryan made a dash for the door.

"Wait!" Nancy shouted. "I'm coming, too!"

Like mini-tornadoes, they were gone, leaving a surprising silence behind them, filled only with the hum of the air conditioner.

"Well, now…I don't have any idea what I'd do with all that energy if I had it." Hamilton Dumas sat down again on the couch, neatly folding the newspapers he'd been reading before he dozed off, and placing them on the coffee table. "Guess that gentleman friend of yours is working today, huh?"

Melinda watched her children out the window, wincing when Ryan stumbled over a curb, then righted himself. She knew her father was talking about Paul, but she wasn't eager to discuss him. "It's a weekday. I assume that's where he is."

"Nice young fellow, that one."

"Everyone seems to think so. His fans are counted in the thousands." The sarcastic retort was beneath her, but she couldn't seem to stop herself. Paul's betrayal, the way he had duped her, still hurt too much.

"Your mother and I thought maybe you and he were getting along pretty good."

To Melinda's dismay, tears welled in her eyes, and the chill of the air-conditioning sent a shiver down her bare arms. Every night for a week, she'd gone to sleep dreaming of Paul, only to wake up with a pillow damp with tears of loss and grief.

"Oh, Daddy, remember those fairy tales you used to read to me about Cinderella and the Sleeping Beauty? I thought when I grew up, someone like you would come along, slide a glass slipper onto my foot, and we'd ride off into the sunset together on a handsome stallion. I got it all wrong, didn't I?" Her choice of Orly had been a disaster—except for the children he'd given her.

Hamilton patted the cushion beside him. "Come here, Mel. Sounds like you've been having a bad day or two. Why don't you tell me all about it?"

Like the little girl she used to be, she sat down beside her father, letting him wrap his arm around her while she rested her head on his shoulder. Funny how she could tell her dad things she'd be embarrassed to reveal to her mother. There was a special bond between them. The heroic cowboy of her childhood had rescued her from more than one mess she'd found herself in.

The summer she turned ten, she'd gotten in over her head in the swimming hole. Her father had dived in after her and pulled her out. When she'd strayed into a pasture with an angry bull, he'd been there to frighten the animal off. And when she'd been feeling her wings in high school, getting in with a bad crowd, he had dragged her back home and given her a lecture she hadn't soon forgotten.

This time, as she related the stunt she'd tried to pull on Paul—and where it had landed her—she didn't think her dad would be able to do much except offer a clean hankie.

"Maybe you've been asking too much of the men in your life," Hamilton suggested when she finally ran out of steam.

She bristled at his lack of sympathy and sat up to look him straight in the eye. "Too much? What do you mean?"

"Those fairy tales were make-believe, pumpkin. By now you should have figured out that real men aren't like that. Chances are, if you've got a problem, you're the only one who can fix it. Not some man with high-flying schemes like Orly. Or some high-priced attorney who'll do most anything to win his case. Zane has been running away from his problems for a long time now. I think maybe you've been doing the same thing."

How on earth did her father think she could *fix* the problems Orly and his shark attorney had caused? She was on the edge of bankruptcy. Running the limo service was barely keeping her head above water, leaving her little time to spend with her children. And to top it all off, her heart was now in tatters.

She pushed herself to her feet. Her father's suggestion stunned her. He'd always been the one person she could count on to take her side. To understand.

Nothing about the mess she was in was her fault.

Hurt by his betrayal, she whirled to march out the door, to go in search of her children, then turned back to her father. He sat there so calmly, his eyes the same shade of light brown as her own, and he looked as though he knew a truth she hadn't yet recognized. Something he'd been trying to teach her for years.

He'd taken her back to that swimming hole and taught her to tread water till her arms and legs ached and she could outswim her brothers. Together they had repaired the downed fence posts that had allowed the bull to wander where he shouldn't have been. Her dad had *forced* her to listen to that long-ago lecture about avoiding trouble, staying away from a bad crowd.

Casually, he picked up his reading glasses from the end table next to a half-full mug of cold coffee and hooked them behind his ears. Something about the gesture made Melinda think he wanted her to see her life—including her foolish mistakes—as clearly as he did, and take responsibility for it.

Dear God! Could he be right?

WHAT LITTLE UNDERGROWTH existed on the eastern slope of the Sierras had dried brown this far into summer, and dust covered the pine trees, turning the needles gray. The sun dipping behind the mountains cast the landscape in muted shadows.

Even so, Paul was optimistic as he drove up the familiar road to the Twin Bar horse ranch. In the past ten days, since he'd last seen Melinda, he'd been busy. He now had a substantial settlement check in his pocket made out to her, and a new, more adequate child-support agreement signed by Orly.

Surely she'd recognize that no matter how wrong he'd been in pretending to believe her whiplash story, his heart had been in the right place. He'd corrected the errors in judgment he'd made, and set things right. They'd be able to start over.

The lights were on as he parked in front of the ranch house, tiny beacons of hope. Melinda, who still hadn't been returning his calls, was home.

AT THE STOVE, Melinda scooped a helping of macaroni and cheese for Ryan, then carried his and Nancy's plates to the kitchen table. The milk was poured, the salad ready.

"Dinner!" she called to the children in the living room.

"Mom! There's somebody here," Nancy yelled.

Frowning, Melinda went to the kitchen doorway just as a pair of headlights switched off outside. They didn't get many visitors. No door-to-door salesmen made the trek up the mountain, and she wasn't expecting company. Particularly at dinnertime.

Ryan popped up from the floor where he'd been playing with his Lego. "I'll see who it is."

"No, you'd better let me," Melinda warned. But it was too late. He'd already thrown the door open.

"Mom! It's Paul!"

Melinda's heart plummeted into her stomach and began to beat wildly. Involuntarily, she lifted her hand to her hair, trying to smooth back the unruly waves. She didn't have on a smidgen of makeup. Her shirt had a rip in the shoulder; her jeans were Goodwill rejects. She rolled her eyes and tried to tell herself it didn't matter.

But, of course, that was another lie.

Paul appeared in the doorway, looking devilishly handsome and entirely too masculine. He'd come from the office, and his white shirt gleamed in the porch light as he hefted Ryan in his arms.

"Hey, champ. I've missed you." He rubbed the top of Ryan's head, mussing his hair. "You, too, kiddo," he said to Nancy.

The child stood demurely looking up at him. "I lost another tooth last night."

"Did you now. Pretty soon you won't have any teeth left at all and you'll have to gum your food like an old granny."

She giggled, and the sound cut right through to Melinda's heart. Her children idolized Paul. He'd won them over with the ease of a magician. But the only one who'd been fooled was Melinda. She'd thought she could love a man, expect him to solve her problems for her, and not be hurt in the process. She'd been so terribly wrong in so many ways. Her desire for revenge had backfired on her.

His gaze snared hers from across the room and held. The heat of a thousand forest fires seemed to crackle between them. In the mountains, fire was both a destructive and a creative force. It turned the hillsides black as death in a flash, destroying everything in its path. But the following spring, life returned again. Stronger. More resilient. The cycle renewed.

He lowered Ryan to the floor. "I hope I haven't come at a bad time."

She struggled to find her voice. "We were just about to have dinner."

"It's mac and cheese," Ryan announced. "You can have some, too, if you want. Mom makes it real good."

"I'm sure she does." Paul's gaze never left hers. "But I just came by to talk to your mom for a few minutes. I've brought some forms for her to sign. I didn't mean to interrupt your dinner."

"It's all right." Curious, Melinda stepped forward. Surely Orly wasn't taking her back to court to reduce his already miniscule child-support payments. She had to believe Paul wouldn't let him pull a stunt like that. "You children go on into the kitchen and eat. Your supper's on your plates."

"But can't Paul stay?" Nancy pleaded.

"You go eat your dinner, kiddo. I'll talk to your mom and maybe she'll let me come back another time."

With obvious reluctance, the children headed for the kitchen.

Paul gestured toward the front door. "It's a nice night out. We could talk on the porch."

His seriousness sent flutters of unease through her midsection. She couldn't possibly afford to hire an attorney to take Orly to court again.

Paul held the door open for her and she stepped outside, careful not to come too close to him. Not to let their arms brush. Even so, she caught the scent of his spicy aftershave before she could put some distance between them.

At the far end of the porch, she stood in the shadows by the railing, looking out over the valley. Through the pine trees, she couldn't make out the glimmer of distant lights, but mostly she was aware of Paul standing inches behind her, and she ached for him to put his arms around her. Kiss her.

As though he were as uneasy as she, as unsure of what would come next, he cleared his throat.

''I need to apologize to you for not doing my job properly as an officer of the court.'' His voice was low, intimate. ''Until Zach told me you didn't own any part of the Twin Bar, I had no idea Orly had lied to me in your divorce case. I believed every word he said. I don't usually think of myself as gullible, but in Orly's case I was.''

''Like you, he can be a very convincing man.''

''The past few weeks I've been doing the research I should have done before the hearing. Based on that, I've persuaded Orly to rethink the original divorce settlement. In fact, in order to avoid being charged with perjury, he has decided generosity is a virtue.''

She turned, confused. ''Generosity? Orly doesn't know the meaning of—''

Paul handed her a check.

In the dim light seeping out from the living room windows, she studied the slim piece of paper, trying to focus on the numbers.

Suddenly she felt shell-shocked, disoriented. Granted, the amount might not be huge for a man like Paul, but to her it represented a new beginning. Independence.

Her head snapped up. "Is this real?"

"A cashier's check. I didn't trust Orly not to stop payment on one of his own."

"This is…it's wonderful." The plans she'd barely laid seemed all the more possible now with a decent nest egg to back her up.

"There's more." He produced a sheaf of papers she hadn't noticed he'd been holding. "With my encouragement, Orly has agreed to up his monthly child-support payments. There are some caveats, because his income does tend to be irregular."

"That's how it is when you gamble on everything from real estate to the gaming tables."

"In any event, the bottom line is about three times what you've been receiving to date."

"Three times!" she gasped. "He'll never pay—"

"He will unless he wants to end up behind bars. I've seen to that. All I need now is your signature on the agreement."

"All I need is a pen." As she reached for the papers and Paul pulled a pen from his pocket, she thought better of the idea. "How 'bout I read them over first in the bright light of day, then send them back to your office?'' For once she intended not to do anything foolish that would get her into deeper trouble than she'd been in for the past year.

''Sure. As soon I get the signed papers back, I'll file them with the court.''

Taking the paperwork, she folded it in her hands, astonished by what Paul had done for her. ''I can't tell you how much I appreciate this. The children—''

''You've got to know there's more than one reason why I wanted to take Orly to task. I needed to right the wrong I'd done to you.''

''You didn't know...''

With his fingertips, he caressed her cheek—so tenderly it almost brought tears to her eyes.

''And I was hoping, if I could make it all right again, that maybe, well, that maybe you and your kids would move back in with me. That we could give it a second shot.''

His offer astonished her. She hadn't been expecting it, and she was rocked back on her heels. He wanted her to move in with him? For real this time? The two of them, together, as if none of this had happened? As though she hadn't concocted a scheme to sue the bejeebers out of him? Never mind that he'd gone along despite knowing the truth.

It would be so damn easy to agree to his suggestion. All of her problems would be solved—at least her financial woes. With Orly's new settlement check and increased child-support payments, she'd be in fat city.

And in Paul's bed, where she'd dearly love to be.

Plus, she'd get to try out that Jacuzzi bubble bath with him, an image that was still haunting her dreams.

But that wouldn't solve her problems, would it? It would simply compound them, because she wouldn't be relying on herself. She'd be relying on a knight in shining armor who could as easily ride out of her life in the same way a prince vanished when you closed the cover on a book of fairy tales.

Gently, aching with regret, she brushed a kiss to his lips.

"I can't move in with you, Paul."

"Why on earth not? It's not like I'm asking you or the kids to be tied down. I'm just looking for a second chance."

Maybe that was the problem. She deserved more than a relationship with a man who didn't offer marriage or love, but only a live-in arrangement. A man who avoided divorce by never getting married.

"I've been doing a lot of thinking in the past couple of weeks," she said. "My father, bless his heart, gave me one of his lectures, and this time I'm going to listen very closely. However much I appreciate Orly's check, I'm the one who has to solve my own problems."

"I'm not following."

She slipped away from him, walked down the steps and out toward the pasture, where the mares were grazing before calling it night. Above her, scattered stars were beginning to appear in the sky. Behind her, Paul's footsteps crunched on the gravel path. She stopped at the fence before turning around.

"You're partly to blame for my decision, you know."

"What decision?"

"I'm selling the limo service. It's been like a millstone around my neck, taking me away from my children and not providing enough income to make a decent living. Typical of Orly's schemes."

"Some of his schemes have worked out better than others," Paul conceded.

"You know, you're like him in a lot of ways. You wanted to win in my divorce case—in all your cases, I suspect—without regard to right or wrong. And that's why you didn't question Orly too closely."

"My job is to represent my clients as vigorously as I can."

"Is it? Or should an attorney have some higher calling?"

Her accusation stunned Paul, forcing him to take a step back. "Now wait a minute."

"The other thing I'm going to do is become a school bus driver while I finish up my college degree in accounting. I've already passed the tests for the school district, and I'll start work when school begins."

"Bus driver?"

"You did it." She looked at him smugly. "I figured what's good enough for you is good enough for me. I'll be able to schedule my classes around the hours I work driving the bus. It may take me a while to get my degree, but at least someday I'll be able to support my kids on my own. Hopefully before they reach old age.''

In disbelief, he shook his head. ''How are you going to commute—''

''Until you brought me this check, I thought I'd have to rent a small place in town. But now…'' She shrugged. ''Maybe I'll be able to put a down payment on a condo. Nothing spectacular, of course, but it would be a place to call our own.''

''You're incredible,'' Paul said with a mixture of admiration and dismay. She was rejecting his offer. Wouldn't be moving in with him, despite all of his efforts to nail Orly to the wall with the truth and make him pay up.

Where the hell had he gone wrong? Paul wondered. He'd been so damn sure she and the kids would move back to his house.

He tried one last argument. He was good at persuading people, damn it. That's what he did for a living!

''You wouldn't have to buy or rent a place if you lived with me. Your costs would be a lot less and you'd be free to come and go. It would make sense—''

''Not to me it wouldn't. Maybe a month ago, but not now. I'm sorry, Paul.''

She'd shut him down. The star of the high school debating team was left with nothing else to say. And he didn't know why that should hurt so damn much. It was only a game, right? Like foosball.

Except it didn't feel that way as Paul drove back down the hill to his upscale house, empty except for a talkative housekeeper who had been giving him hell ever since Melinda and the kids moved out.

CHAPTER TWELVE

STANDING IN THE LOBBY of Paul's office building, Melinda waited with Natalie for the elevator to arrive. "I think it's a mistake for me to come with you."

"I don't want to face Rocky alone."

"You won't be alone. Paul will be there. He's a shark. As long as he's representing you, you'll be just fine."

Natalie took Melinda's hand and squeezed her fingers. Her palm was sweaty. Or maybe Melinda was the one who was sweating. A week had passed since Paul had brought her the new divorce settlement, and there hadn't been a day Melinda wasn't tempted to call him, tell him she and her children would be waiting for him when he got home from the office. And in their first private moment, she wanted to make use of that bubble bath he'd purchased.

It had taken every bit of her willpower not to make that call.

"Having a good attorney is one thing," Natalie said. "And I'm glad Paul was willing to take my case. But there's no man in the world who can understand what it's like for a woman to face the fact that her marriage has failed. Even when her husband *is* a jerk.''

''That's true enough.'' Melinda's own divorce had demoralized her. Her sense of self had taken a full year to recover. Only now did she feel strong enough to move forward on her own.

What ironic timing that this was the moment she'd found someone to love.

The elevator pinged and the doors swished open, allowing two well-dressed businessmen to exit. Still Melinda hesitated to step inside. How would she be able to hide her emotions from Paul? Not let him see she was desperately weak and wanted him to ask her to move in with him again?

''I need you, Mel.'' Natalie held the elevator door open. ''I promise I won't let Paul attack you.''

But can you promise I won't jump his bones? Sighing, Melinda lifted her chin and stepped into the elevator.

ROCKY GREENE and his attorney, Marc Oggleberry, were already in the conference room. But Paul wanted to wait until Natalie arrived, make sure she was calm and clear about what would take place at the meeting. That he would do all the talking. She simply had to be there. He'd take care of the rest.

Myrna buzzed him. ''Mrs. Greene is here,'' she said.

''Thanks. I'll be right out.'' He tugged his suit jacket from the hanger in the closet and pulled it on, picking up Natalie's file as he left his office. He'd reviewed all the information that morning. The numbers and what Natalie should expect in a settlement were clear in his mind.

Until he stepped into the reception area and saw Melinda waiting with Natalie.

Then his mind went completely blank, and all he could think about was the way Melinda's hair curled at her chin, the soft blush on her cheeks, and how much he wanted to hold her again. Wearing a simple sheath dress with a light jacket, she looked businesslike. Unapproachable. He liked her better in jeans or a swimsuit. That red silk nightgown. Or better yet, wearing nothing at all.

"I hope you don't mind that I brought Melinda along for moral support," Natalie said.

"Hello," Melinda said softly.

He blinked, nodded and tried to shift back into gear. "It's fine. No problem." Except he was going to have a devil of a time concentrating on the issues in the case instead of what he wanted to do with Melinda.

He stumbled through his instructions to Natalie, reassuring her that he had everything under control. And he did, as far as her case was concerned. But not the Ping-Pong jumping of his own emotions. Damn, he wished they could start over. Wipe out the whole past year and begin again.

He led them into the conference room, introduced Oggleberry to the ladies and offered coffee or soft drinks, which everyone declined. Then they got down to business.

"Before we get too far into the settlement issues," Oggleberry said in his usual pompous manner, "there have been some changes in my client's financial status that you need to be aware of."

Leaning back in his chair, Paul let Oggleberry wax on about Rocky's sudden unemployment and the bad investments he'd made. He'd already checked Greene's financial records and knew what they were up to. Oggleberry was a damn good attorney, a worthy adversary, but Paul wasn't going to let him get away with cheating Natalie out of what was rightfully hers. He wasn't planning to steal Rocky blind, either. *This* time Paul had done his homework.

When Oggleberry finally ran out of steam, Paul flipped open his file and slid a copy of the Greenes' financial records across the table to him. There was only one way to counter Oggleberry's strategy. Paul knew that, because he'd occasionally used the same strategy himself.

"Gentlemen, we're going to come up with a fair settlement here, and I suggest Mr. Greene get himself reemployed in a hurry. Mrs. Greene is not going to be left destitute after a twelve-year marriage. With the help of the courts, I personally plan to see to it."

With that, Paul proceeded to go over the details of the assets involved and exactly how those assets would be distributed.

Watching Oggleberry work the case was like holding up a mirror to himself, and it wasn't a pretty picture. Win at all costs. Represent the client without seeking balance or being fair. Gain yourself the reputation of being the best damn divorce attorney in the state.

Shame raked through Paul. Melinda had been right. There had to be a lot of ex-wives who would feel totally justified if they could get even with him.

But never again, he told himself. Even if he'd lost all chance of having Melinda, he was a changed man. He was going to go back through his records, starting with the Short case, the wife who had badgered Myrna about the support payments. In his zeal to defend his clients, he may have overlooked the bigger truth Melinda had talked about—fairness.

FROM HER SEAT beside Natalie, Melinda was fascinated by Paul's command of the situation, the way he wouldn't knuckle under to the other attorney's demands. In an odd way, she loved him for his vigorous defense of Natalie's interests even more than she'd hated him during her own divorce proceedings.

His reputation as the best divorce attorney in the state was well deserved.

"You're taking me to the cleaners," Rocky complained as the meeting wound down.

"You should have thought of that before you decided you wanted out of the marriage," Natalie said calmly.

Rocky glared at Melinda. "It sure didn't cost Orly an arm and a leg when he dumped his old lady."

She gave him a smug smile. "Bet you haven't talked to him lately." Not since Paul had made her ex sign the new agreement. Orly had to be spitting tacks by now.

"All right, I think we've settled most of the issues." Paul stood to end the meeting. "I'll have my secretary write up the agreement and send a courier with it to your office tomorrow."

Rocky sputtered another complaint, this time to his lawyer. "I thought you were gonna get me a good deal, man. You're gonna leave me with nothin'."

Oggleberry took his client by the arm and escorted him out the door, not bothering to thank Paul for his hospitality. He had the look of a beaten man.

Melinda smiled to herself.

Turning to Natalie, Paul asked, "Are you going to be all right?"

"There'll be some adjustments, but the kids and I will be fine, thanks to you."

He shook her hand, then glanced past Natalie to Melinda. "And you're going to be okay now, too?"

"Yes." As soon as she could find some glue that would hold her heart together. "I start my bus driving job the middle of next week, and I've enrolled in a couple of classes at the university for the fall."

"That's good."

"We still have to find another place to live."

He let the comment hang there a moment before saying, "Let me know if there's anything I can do to help."

Her mouth felt dry and she swallowed hard. "I will." Somehow they'd gone from enemies to friends with only a brief interlude as lovers. She wished that space of time had lasted longer.

"Well, then..." Natalie stepped away. "You two probably have lots to talk about. And I need to get home. I'll just run along—"

"I'm coming with you." Melinda hastened to leave with her friend. She didn't dare stay with Paul. Every bit of her resolve to become independent, to depend only on herself, would fall by the wayside.

She couldn't even find her voice to tell him good-bye.

Her flight stopped in front of the elevator doors, where Natalie punched the call button.

"My lord, Melinda, I thought that conference room was going to catch on fire the way you two were looking at each other." Grinning foolishly, Natalie fanned her hand in front of her face.

"I don't know what you're talking about."

"You don't? Well, I tell you, I've never seen a man look more like he wanted to drag a woman off to his cave and make wild passionate love. When are you two going to get back together?"

"We're not." Tapping her toe impatiently, she waited for the elevator to show up. "And if you saw something in there, I'm sure it was nothing more than a good dose of lust."

"You're kidding, right?"

The elevator arrived with a ping; the doors opened. Inside, a woman and two men stood waiting, all of them carrying briefcases, no doubt attorneys from some other office in the building.

Melinda entered, then turned to face the door. ''No, I'm not kidding.''

''Honestly, Melinda, if you can't see it, I certainly can. Paul DeMarco is a desperate man and he's in love with you.''

The heat of a blush rushed up Melinda's neck, feeling like the desert sun at high noon. It wasn't possible that Paul loved her. *Wanted* her, yes. She wouldn't deny that. But he'd made it abundantly clear he didn't believe in romantic love.

Given her history, she didn't imagine she could be the one to persuade him otherwise.

And had it really been necessary for Natalie to announce her faulty conclusion to the entire Reno legal community?

PRACTICALLY THE ENTIRE family descended on him that weekend. Paul wasn't in the mood for company. They didn't seem to care.

While the kids were in the pool, supervised by his brothers-in-law, his sisters and mother cornered him in the living room.

Olivia perched on the arm of a chair. ''We want to know why Melinda moved out.''

Paul tried to escape the room, but Angela, holding little Pauline in her arms, blocked his way.

''I don't think that's any of your business,'' he said.

''We want to know what you did to her,'' Angela insisted.

''I didn't do anything. For God's sake, I—''

"Of course you did." Olivia got in his face, her dark eyes flashing. "You scared her off, didn't you? Came on too strong, right?"

"Hardly." Things hadn't been like this when they were growing up. His sisters had looked up to him. Respected him. Not interfered in his life—at least, not often. In return, he'd watched out for them, taking responsibility when they needed his help. Being both a brother and father to them as best he could.

Sitting serenely on the couch knitting a sweater for the baby, his mother said, "Girls, please. Give the poor boy a chance to explain himself."

"I don't have to explain—"

"We all like Melinda very much." His mother set her knitting aside. "And her children. We thought at last you'd found the right woman and that you would marry her."

"Oh, come on, Mama. You know I don't ever plan to marry."

Her brows shot up. "Never?"

"Why on earth not?" Angela demanded.

"Because—"

"The rest of us are happily married," Olivia pointed out. "What makes you think you wouldn't be, too? With the right woman."

"It's not that." He didn't want to argue that in his business he'd seen more marriages fail than survive. "You and Angela were too young to remember how it was after Dad died."

"What does Dad have to do with you chasing off Melinda?" Angela asked.

He glanced at his mother, remembering the heartache. The grief. And the way he hadn't been able to do anything to fix it. ''Every night for weeks after Dad died, I heard Mama crying. I swore on our father's grave that I'd never put any woman through that. And I'm not going to change my mind now.'' His mother still had his dad's framed picture on the table by her bed. She hadn't forgotten and neither could Paul.

Olivia stammered, ''Why—why that's a ridiculous reason to never—''

''Girls.'' His mother stood. ''I want you both to go outside now. See to your children.''

''But, Mama,'' Olivia objected.

''Go,'' she said softly, but in a voice that demanded obedience even though they were themselves grown women with children of their own.

Paul wanted to get out of there, too. ''Look, Mama, I'm sorry. I've got to—''

''No, you need to listen to me and listen to me well.''

He grimaced. She hadn't taken that tone with him since he'd been a boy. ''Mama, you don't understand.''

''I think maybe for the first time I understand why you've avoided marriage and starting a family of your own for so long.''

''I've got a *huge* family. All the nieces and nephews I could possibly handle.'' And two more sisters than he wanted at this point. Thank goodness his brother, Carl, hadn't gotten into the act, too.

His mother looked Paul straight in the eye as though she weren't a good five inches shorter than him. "Do you believe that if I had known before we got married that your father would pass away so early in life, I would have given up one day, one *minute* of the time I was given to be together with him?"

"Well, no, but you couldn't have known."

"If I had, I would have married him sooner."

Paul scowled, but he couldn't escape her penetrating eyes. "You cried yourself sick."

"I know. Even now I sometimes miss him so much that it hurts."

"See? That's what I'm saying. No woman should have to live with that kind of a loss."

"Oh, my sweet little boy," she crooned, almost laughing. "You were so young when your father died, and so eager to be the man of the house. But I failed to teach you the most important thing about women."

"What's that?"

"If a woman can go to her grave knowing she was well loved, then she is a happy woman. Losing a man she loves is dreadful. But never having experienced that kind of love is far worse."

He shook his head. Despite having two sisters and a mother, he knew he'd never figure out women.

"Paul, do you love Melinda?"

He opened his mouth to deny the possibility and then snapped it closed. For the life of him, he wasn't sure. He missed her like crazy. Her smile. Her laughter. He definitely wanted her in his bed.

But love? That was something outside his experience. He'd always kept women at an emotional arm's length. Had Melinda slipped past his defenses while he wasn't looking?

"I don't know, Mama."

She patted his cheek. "Think about it, son. If you do love her—and I suspect that's what's made you so melancholy since she left—then you must find a way to tell her. I think you may find she loves you, too."

Paul didn't think either of those scenarios was possible. Melinda had moved out. She'd rejected the notion of coming back. She wanted to be independent, damn it!

Despite his conviction that he couldn't be in love with Melinda, the possibility stuck like a bone caught in his throat. He couldn't get rid of the idea for the rest of the weekend.

And when he realized he was well and truly snagged, he couldn't figure out what to do about it. Convincing Melinda he was not only a changed man but one who could leave her plenty of leeway to be as independent as she wanted in marriage would require desperate measures.

By Monday he'd finally come up with a plan. He gave Tilly the day off—insisted, in fact, that she go shopping and see a movie. Play blackjack at a casino, if she wanted to. He'd foot the bill.

When he arrived at his office, he went striding past

Stacy in the reception area and headed right for Myrna's desk.

"I'd like you to call Advanced Limo Service. I want a driver named Melinda to pick me up in—" he glanced at his watch "—a half hour in front of Harrah's Hotel."

"Has your car broken down, Mr. D? I could loan you mine."

"No, that's not my problem." Something far more serious was involved. His entire future. "Give her a phony name—Smith or something."

Myrna looked at him as though he'd lost his mind.

"And don't give her the name of the law firm, okay?"

"Where shall I say Mr. Smith wants to go?"

"Someplace expensive. Far enough away that she can't turn down the job."

Still eyeing him suspiciously, Myrna said, "How 'bout Tahoe for the day?"

"Perfect. Make the call. And be sure the driver's name is Melinda." He'd have to hope he hadn't come to his senses too late, that she hadn't sold the limo business yet and was off training for her bus driver's job.

Damn, how had he been so stupid not to realize he'd fallen in love with her the moment she'd walked into his conference room more than a year ago?

CHAPTER THIRTEEN

THE DOWNTOWN RENO TRAFFIC seemed particularly heavy for a Monday morning.

Melinda had trouble maneuvering the limo toward the taxi curb at Harrah's. If she'd gotten the call for this run tomorrow, she would have been on her new job, learning the school bus route. As it was, she'd planned to spend the day doing some house hunting. In both cases, her children had groused about being left on their own at the ranch with dear, long-suffering Ramón.

But an all-day jaunt to Tahoe was simply too lucrative to turn down.

Keeping one eye on the traffic and the other watching for a signal from the hotel doorman, she edged the limo forward. Just as she did, a man stepped off the curb. Right in front of her!

She had only a quick glimpse of him before she slammed on her brakes. Then he vanished out of sight beneath the wheels of her limousine!

"Oh, my God!" Panic rocketed through her as she stopped and leaped from the vehicle. She'd been in only one car accident in her life—that fender bender. Now, on her last day in the business, she'd hit a pedestrian.

A small crowd quickly gathered around the fallen man.

"Is he all right? How badly is he hurt?" She pushed her way past a uniformed doorman and abruptly halted. Her jaw dropped and she blinked, unbelieving. "Paul?" Grief, so sharp it forced her to her knees, overwhelmed her. He was so still, crumpled there at the curb as though—

He groaned.

The breath she'd been holding escaped her lungs in a whoosh. Thank heavens he wasn't dead.

"Someone call an ambulance," she cried. "We've got to get him to the hospital."

"No, no," he moaned, raising his hand to stop her frantic pleas for help. He looked a little dazed, but no blood was apparent. "I'm all right. Just bruised. Nothing's broken. Maybe my neck..." He groaned again.

Melinda was struck by a powerful sense of déjà vu. She'd been distracted. She hadn't noticed him standing on the curb. He'd stepped out of nowhere exactly as though he had *staged* the accident.

Frowning, trying to figure out what that meant, she sat back on her haunches.

The doorman leaned forward. "Do you want me to call an ambulance, sir? The paramedics can be here in minutes. It might be the wisest—"

"No, I think maybe this young lady can help me with my injuries." He raised himself on one elbow. "What do you think, Melinda? Have you got a cure for my ills?"

She gazed into chocolate-brown eyes filled with sincerity, and for the first time saw uncertainty. He wasn't sure what her answer would be, and had gone to a great deal of trouble, not to mention some personal risk, to make sure she'd be hard-pressed to say no.

"I was supposed to pick up a Mr. Smith," she ventured cautiously.

"I know. I'm Mr. Smith. I got tired of you not answering my calls."

She lifted a brow. The entire incident had been a performance, the actor more skilled in the art of making love than in staging a phony street drama. Even so, the lengths he'd gone to thrilled her. Surely it meant he was interested in more than a brief affair.

So was she!

With the help of her father, she'd learned she didn't need a man to rescue her or solve her problems. She was well on her way to doing that for herself and her children. Her feet were firmly planted on the first step to the future.

What she did need was a man to love forever, one who could love and respect her as an equal, as her parents did each other. She could survive without that, but there'd always be an empty spot in her life.

Maybe, just maybe, with a little convincing, Paul was ready to fill that hole in her heart—and let her complete his life with a family of his own.

Glancing up at the doorman, she said, "Could you help me get him into my limo? I know exactly what to do with this gentleman."

She and the doorman each took one of Paul's arms, hauling him to his feet. He staggered, but not convincingly.

"You'll let me know if we're hurting you, won't you?" She suppressed a grin.

"You're being very kind," he mumbled as he slid into the back seat of the limo.

"I think a soak in a Jacuzzi will fix you right up, sir. What do you think?"

His head snapped around and he looked at her. "Jacuzzi?"

"I understand bubble bath has all sorts of curative properties." Gently, she closed the door and circled the limo, getting in behind the wheel.

He rapped his knuckles on the sliding privacy window that separated the driver from the passengers. His mouth moved but she couldn't hear what he said.

Glancing in the rearview mirror, she smiled and switched on the intercom. "Don't worry about a thing, Mr. Smith. I know exactly what needs to be done." Then she pulled away from the curb, heading toward the ritziest suburb in Reno.

DUSTING A FEW SPECKS of dirt from his slacks, Paul leaned back to enjoy the ride. The little minx had figured out his act and had effectively kidnapped him. His plan couldn't be going better.

Except he'd lost control of the situation.

As much as he was eager to share the Jacuzzi with Melinda, they needed to talk. She needed to understand that he loved her. That he wanted her as his wife.

The limo sped through town, a little too fast, he thought. Wallowing Wally needed new shock absorbers, and Paul was feeling slightly nauseous. Or maybe that was just his nerves acting up. He'd never proposed to a woman before.

They made the last turn on his street and she pulled up into his driveway. He struggled with the door handle but she opened it first.

"Here we are, sir. Safe and sound."

"Melinda, I think this chauffeur business has gone far enough. We need to talk."

Hooking her arm through his, she walked him toward the front door. "I do hope you're not planning to sue me. You see, I know this really good attorney, and I promise you, he wouldn't let you get a dime."

"If you're talking about me, I don't do personal injury cases."

"With a little study, I'm sure you'll be able to handle it." She stopped at the door, cocking her head at him. "You do have the key, don't you? Or should I ring for Tilly?"

"Oh, right." Flustered, he'd forgotten about opening the door. All he wanted to do was kiss Melinda. Right there on the porch, and then take her inside. Have his way with her. She looked so darn sexy in that cute little cap, a bow tie pinned at her shirt collar. "As a matter of fact, I gave Tilly the whole day off."

Melinda's eyes crinkled when she smiled. ''How very convenient, Mr. Smith.''

He fumbled in his trouser pocket for the key. His fingers were all-thumbs, and his hand trembled as he tried to slide the key into the lock.

''Hmm, let me.''

She covered his hand with hers, her fingers dainty yet competent, her nails neatly trimmed. Together they opened the door and stepped inside. Even though the air conditioner was on, sweat beaded Paul's forehead.

''Melinda, honey, let's—''

''Let's get you upstairs. Nothing like a good, hot soak in a tub, right? Wouldn't want your muscles to tighten up after a bad accident like that.''

She snared him by his tie, gently tugging him up the stairs. He went willingly enough. No matter what she did, no matter what she had in mind, he wouldn't be able to resist her.

In the bathroom, she turned on the water in the tub. ''Where's that bubble bath you bought?''

''In the drawer. But aren't we moving a little fast here?''

She poured a half cup of liquid into the fast-flowing water. Bubbles rose along with the scent of wintergreen. She slipped his jacket from his shoulders.

''Melinda?'' His voice caught. She was going to seduce him, and he was helpless to stop her. A prisoner of her innocent wiles. ''You're killing me, sweetheart.''

''Oh, I hope not.'' Deftly, her fingers loosened his

tie and worked the buttons on his shirtfront. "I have something very special in mind for you, and I want you very much alive."

He was alive, all right. Achingly so.

She unhooked his belt buckle and unsnapped his pants, slowly lowering his zipper.

He groaned, not faking the pain now.

"You know, if you'd misjudged your dive off the curb, I really might have run over you." Spreading his shirt open, she pressed a kiss to his chest, then ran her tongue down the tanned skin.

Capturing her head in his hands, he lifted her face, kissing her long and hard, hungrily plunging his tongue into the cavern of her mouth. She tasted of mischief and hot, sweet peppermint. Her chauffeur's cap slipped off her head, plopping lightly on the tile floor. Wildly, he struggled to get her jacket off, too.

"Not yet," she whispered against his lips, pushing him away. "First, it's your turn to be taken care of. Nothing better for your aches and pains than a whirlpool and a massage." Her eyes gleamed, filled with the promise of playful revenge.

A game he was sure to lose.

While steam rose from the tub, she stripped him naked. He'd never been so hot. So eager to have a woman in his arms. *This* woman. No other would do.

He wondered if she had any idea how arousing her seduction was, although the evidence was more than apparent as he stepped into the tub in response to her command.

"You know I'm going to get back at you for this, don't you?" he said.

"I most assuredly hope so."

As he sat down, she knelt beside the tub, found a washcloth and began to swirl it across his chest. He caught her wrist.

"If we're going to do this, we're going to do it right." He slipped the cloth from her hand. "I want to feel you touching me. All over."

Her eyes widened. "A glutton for punishment, huh?"

"*Your* kind of punishment." He gritted his teeth and tried to hold on as she tortured him with her hands.

Melinda felt as though she were on fire. Her heart pounded in her throat, and she could barely catch her breath. Beneath the blanket of bubbles, her fingers closed around his hard velvet shaft.

Oh, my… He wanted her; she had no doubt of that. And she wanted him. Her womb pulsed with the knowledge.

His eyes narrowed, and a muscle flexed in his jaw, echoing the jerk of his arousal, which she felt in her hand. "Your jacket's getting soaked."

"It doesn't matter."

"Take your clothes off, honey. Join me in here. There's plenty of room."

She was beyond the teasing mood that had started all this. She wanted more. She wanted to feel the length of him along her body, his heat inside her, throbbing where she needed him the most.

Forgetting that she had set off on this seductive game, she shrugged out of her wet jacket, tossing it aside. Next came her blouse, which she flung carelessly across the room. After shedding her shoes, she hopped from one foot to the other, ridding herself of her slacks.

All the time he watched her, his dark eyes never leaving her, though she knew her striptease was anything but graceful. It didn't matter. Not to her. Not to Paul.

Stepping into the tub, she knelt, straddling him. The water surged around her, bubbles sweeping across her breasts as she bent to kiss him. The sensation was dizzying, his heat and the water mixing in a passionate swirl of desire.

This was where she belonged. In his arms. In his life. However long he wanted her there. Not because he could solve all of her problems or rescue her from her own mistakes.

But because she loved him.

They kissed and caressed, hands and lips exploring, until the water cooled. And still they held back from the ultimate intimacy. What they both wanted.

Lifting her from the tub, Paul wrapped Melinda in a fluffy towel and carried her to his bed, tossing back the covers before he lowered her onto it.

"You are so beautiful," he whispered.

"So are you, my love." Reaching up to him, she welcomed him into her embrace.

When he entered her, he did so with tenderness, a sense of coming home. A peace settled over her even as he aroused her beyond all measure. His rhythm matched her own, capturing her in a perfect partnership.

His name snagged in her throat when she reached the peak. She sobbed as he filled her again, then she spun out of control, her body pulsing as she drew him ever more deeply within her.

"Mel!" he rasped, holding her tightly as he found his own release in her arms.

They lay wrapped together for a long time, his weight on top of her, her fingertips caressing his shoulder, the length of his spine, toying with the hair at his nape.

The bright midday sun sharpened the images in the room: a reading lamp beside the bed; a big chest of drawers in a rich, dark wood; Paul pressed against her, the man she loved.

At last he lifted his weight and rolled to the side, one arm still around her.

"As soon as I'm able to think straight," he said, "I've got a couple of things to say."

She tucked her head on his shoulder, resting her hand on his stomach. He had a flat abdomen, a neat little innie belly button.

"It seems to me we've had an interesting conversation for the past hour or so." She let her hand slip lower.

"Don't start. Please," he gasped. "I can't think when you do that."

She giggled. So much the better. She didn't want to hear him say he didn't believe in love and marriage. She didn't want to feel the resulting shaft of pain.

He caught her hand. "I love you and I want to marry you."

Her body went utterly still. She couldn't draw a breath. She didn't think her heart was even capable of beating. Struggling to regain her faculties, she said, "I thought you didn't believe in—"

"I didn't. But you changed me, Mel. I think that change started the moment you first walked into my office, but I was too dumb—or scared—to recognize it."

She turned to look at him. "And now?"

"I'm more scared that I'll lose you. I swear I'm not the same attorney I used to be. Winning at all cost isn't going to be the name of the game anymore."

She knew that was true. She'd seen it with her own eyes at Natalie's conference. Paul had been firm but not out for blood from the opposing side.

"And I know you want to be independent," he continued, his voice as determined as it would be when defending a case in court.

"I do want to get my degree. I've finally realized an education is like an insurance policy. A woman shouldn't be without one."

"I can understand that, after what you went through with your ex. In fact, I totally agree. And I can wait as long as you want me to, if I have to." He brushed a kiss on her palm. "You and the kids can live here while you're going to school or whatever you have to do. Or you can live on your own for a while. But I want to know *someday* you'll be my wife.''

His proposal stunned her. She'd never expected…

In a rush, before he could change his mind, she gave him the answer she longed to give. ''Yes.''

''Yes?''

''Yes, I'll marry you. I don't know quite when. Or where I'll live for now. I have the children to think about.''

''There's a school right down the street, within walking distance. And Tilly would be here to baby-sit. As long as we have adjoining rooms, it could work out. We could be discreet.''

His offer was more than tempting. ''I doubt we'd fool anyone, not even the children. What would our families think?''

''My family threatened me with mayhem if I didn't ask you to marry me.''

''They didn't!''

''Well, not exactly. But close.'' Rising above her, he kissed her softly. Gently. Sealing the bargain. ''I'm going to get you the biggest diamond ring I can find in Reno so everyone will know you're going to be my wife.''

''You don't have to do that.'' She kissed him back, tasting her own flavor on his lips as well as his. ''Knowing you love me is all that matters.''

''How 'bout you? Do you think you could, in time—''

''Love you?''

He nodded, his forehead furrowing with concern. A confident man no longer so sure of himself.

"That's been a done deal for a long time, Mr. Hotshot Attorney. Why else do you think I'd drag you back to your own lair to seduce you?"

"I dunno." He shrugged. "Because I'm a great lover?"

Laughing, she tweaked his earlobe. "I won't deny that. But more important, you're the man I *love.* The whole package."

As though he'd expended every bit of his energy, he collapsed back onto his pillow. "Thank God for that."

"I love you, Paul DeMarco. I promise I always will." She trailed her fingers down the center of his chest, teasingly close to that amazing part of his anatomy that had recently given her so much pleasure. Instantly, it responded. "When do you think we ought to tell the children and our respective families?"

"Woman," he groaned, "if you keep doing that, I'm never going to have the strength to get out of this bed to tell anyone."

For now, that's exactly what she had in mind. Her own sweet revenge on him for having put her through such misery, making her believe he'd never consider love and marriage. And she intended to enjoy every minute of getting even.

THE MOMENT MELINDA'S mother opened the door of her town house, Nancy dashed inside.

''Grandma! We're getting married!''

''Oh, my gracious, child!'' Eleanor Dumas glanced at Melinda and Paul standing on the front step, and smiled. ''Aren't you too young to get married?'' she teased her granddaughter.

''No, not me, Grandma. It's Mom and Paul who are getting married.''

''Ah, how lovely.''

''I get to be best man,'' Ryan announced solemnly.

''And I get to be a bridesmaid! And Aunt Olivia will do up my hair and fix my fingernails. Paul says so.''

Hard-pressed to keep her excitement under control, Melinda said, ''We haven't told Olivia about her duties yet. We wanted you to hear the news first.''

''My goodness, that is exciting, isn't it? Come in, all of you.'' Eleanor opened the door wide.

''I get to be the one to tell Grandpa.'' Ryan barreled past his sister, although he didn't win the race by much.

Laughing, Melinda stepped into her mother's outstretched arms.

''Oh, darling, I'm so happy for you.'' Tears shone in Eleanor's eyes. ''My baby girl.''

''Hardly that, Mother.'' Although she did feel it had taken a long while to finally grow up and accept responsibility for her own happiness.

''Am I allowed to kiss my son-in-law to be?''

''Absolutely.'' Paul bent to give Eleanor a hug

and brushed a kiss to her cheek. "I feel like I'm the luckiest man in the world that Melinda has agreed to marry me. I was scared to death that she'd turn me down."

Eleanor laughed. "My daughter is smarter than that!"

Hamilton Dumas appeared from upstairs, tugged along by Nancy and Ryan. "I hear there's going to be a wedding," he said.

Melinda hugged her father. It didn't take long before everyone in the room was crying, with the notable exception of Ryan, who thought crying was a sissy thing to do. The tears that sheened Paul's eyes might have changed his mind, however. Melinda knew they brought a lump to her throat, making her realize again what a strong, caring man she'd agreed to marry.

Then Melinda showed off her ring, a full-carat diamond solitaire surrounded by tiny sapphires. Paul had gone shopping for the ring the morning after his proposal, while she'd been training for her new bus driver's job. He'd presented it to her that evening wrapped inside a silk nightie the same color as the sapphires. She didn't know which gift was more extravagant. But based on the evening she'd spent with Paul, she figured she was likely to get a lot more wear out of the ring than the nightie.

"So tell us," her mother asked, after admiring the ring, "when will the big day happen?"

"We're not sure yet," Melinda admitted.

"I'm pressing for as soon as possible," Paul said.

"This weekend would suit me just fine. But I'm willing to wait if that's what makes Melinda happy. For a while, at any rate."

"We haven't quite decided where to live—I mean, until the wedding."

"I wanna live at Paul's house," Ryan declared.

"Me, too," Nancy agreed.

Melinda glanced at her parents.

"You're a grown woman, dear," her mother said. "I know when I fell in love with your father, I didn't waste any time worrying about what other people might think." She took her husband's hand, the glow of fifty years of devotion in her eyes. "I suspect both Hamilton and I remember what it was like to fall in love. We both simply want our children to be happy. We won't ever ask for more than that."

Her father nodded. "Seems to me we're getting that wish for Zach, now that Leslie has pretty well hog-tied him. I'm happy for you, too, Mel. I think you've got yourself a good man there."

"Thank you, sir," Paul said. The two men shook hands.

Eleanor sighed. "Now, if only Zane could find his way back home from wherever he is, and put his grief behind him."

"He will, Mom," Melinda said. "It's just a question of time."

"Can we go back over to Paul's house now?" Ryan asked. "I want to go swimming."

"It's almost your bedtime."

"Aw, Mom."

Paul slid his arm around her waist. ''They could stay over. Sleep late.''

She could see exactly what he was thinking, and hated to be the one to pop his bubble. ''I have to get up early in the morning. Another day of training.''

''I can see right now, life is going to get complicated married to a career woman. The sacrifices we men have to make.''

Laughing, Melinda elbowed him in the ribs. ''Come on, kids. Paul's house it is.''

After they said good-night to her folks and shared more hugs, they set out for Paul's house. In no time, the children were in the pool, stirring up the water like an excited school of fish.

Melinda and Paul sat together on a padded chaise longue, watching them. In the evening sky, the setting sun caught a jet contrail, turning it into a pink streak across the heavens.

Suddenly, tears of happiness flooded Melinda's eyes. ''We're going to be all right, aren't we? The four of us.''

''I promise. Except I thought maybe, if you were willing, someday there could be five or six of us.''

''Five or six?''

He framed her face with his big, gentle hands. ''I already love your kids as though they were my own. But I'd like you to consider having more children with me.''

''Oh, Paul, I hadn't thought that far.'' The tears that had welled in her eyes spilled down her cheeks.

"I can't think of anything I'd like more than to have your babies."

"Thank you." Slowly, he lowered his head and kissed her, ever so tenderly.

She leaned into him, relishing the sensation of being home after a long, lonely journey.

"Look! Mommy's kissing Paul!" Ryan chortled.

"She's supposed to. They're in love," Nancy explained.

Beneath Paul's lips, Melinda smiled. Her little girl was growing up far too fast.

The sliding glass door to the house opened. Tilly called to the children in a stage whisper, "Come on, you two youngsters. I made brownies. Come inside and eat them. We'll leave your mother and Mr. D alone."

When they'd all gone inside, Melinda curled up beside Paul on the lounge and sighed. "Have I told you lately how much I love you?"

"I'm a very insecure fellow. Tell me again."

"I love you, Paul DeMarco."

"I love you, too, my future Mrs. D."

He kissed her again, and Melinda knew her life would be filled with all the love she could handle. She intended to return the favor in full measure.

It was by far the best revenge she could imagine.

Look forward to all these wonderful books this Christmas

XMAS/LIST